Finding Love In The Right Places

5 Short Stories of Finding Love

C S Farabee

Farabee Publishing
Arizona

This book is a work of fiction. Names, Characters, places, and incidents either are the product of the author's imagination or are used fictitiously, and any resemblance to actual persons living or dead, business establishments, events or locals is entirely coincidental.

Farabee Publishing
Chandler, AZ 85224
www.Farabeepublishing.com

Copyright 2006 by CS Farabee
All rights reserved. This book, or parts thereof, may not be reproduced in any form without permission.

ISBN: 978-1-63760-820-3

Printed in the United States of America

Book Cover designed by: David Mor

Keep Your Face To The Sunshine

"Keep your face to the sunshine and you cannot see the shadows. It is what the sunflowers do."
Helen Keller

To Everyone that believes in Love and for those that need more convincing

Cassie was born unable to speak. She never cried but thrashed around in her bed when she was hungry. Cassie's mother, Rebecca, knew her husband would not be pleased about Cassie not being able to speak. She hid it from him for as long as she could. He just thought she was a quiet child. Cassie would be looked at as mentally ill and he would want to send her away.

Rebecca sent for a book, she had heard about, that contained hand signs, that allowed those that could not speak to communicate. She taught Cassie the hand signs and they communicated. Cassie was very bright for three years old and would ask questions with her hands. It did not take her long to understand the hand signs.

Rebecca's husband, Charles, came across them one day when Cassie and Rebecca were signing with their hands. He stared at Cassie and now knew why he had never heard any noise from her. He was angry at Rebecca. "Rebecca. Why did you keep this from me?"

Cassie and Rebecca both jumped at the sound of his harsh tone.

Rebecca stood and faced her husband. "Because you would have sent her away. She is very bright and does not belong in some institution for the mentally ill."

Charles looked at Cassie. She seemed like a normal little girl. Her blond hair framed her chubby face and she looked at him with wide blue eyes.

He looked back at his wife. "Can she at least hear?"

Rebecca nodded. "Yes. We use sign language so that she can speak to me. But she can hear."

Charles turned to Cassie. "Can you hear me? If so tell me your name."

Cassie signed her name and smiled at him.

Charles looked at Rebecca. "She signed her name."

Charles sighed and left the room. Rebecca was pregnant and he did not want to upset her, but he would have to watch Cassie. If she showed any signs of mental imbalance he would have to send her away. He hoped for a son this time and would not jeopardize his son's well being. No matter what the cost.

Rebecca gave Charles his son four months later. Charles was happy but watched Cassie closely. She was not allowed near his son.

As Cassie grew older Charles began to relax when he saw there was no sign of her being mentally ill. He did not learn the sign language and spoke to her very little.

Rebecca taught Cassie to read and write. She would spend hours in the library, of their home, reading stories and signing questions to her mother. Little Jonathan was taught to sign so that he could talk to his sister. Charles was not comfortable with this but said nothing.

Cassie did not have many friends. When they found out she could not speak they would call her names and stayed away from her. By the time she was eighteen she knew that she would never marry. No man would want a wife that could not speak.

Rebecca had given him three more children over the years, and he did not want the burden of taking care of Cassie all her life. He knew he could not marry her off. So, he decided for her to go west to live with his brother, on his ranch in Texas. He needed a cook and Cassie would do well there. If nothing else she was a hard worker.

Rebecca was heartsick at the thought of Cassie going out into the world alone and not being able to speak to anyone.

Charles would not hear her arguments and planned for Cassie to leave the following week.

Cassie was to take the train and then a stagecoach to the Circle T ranch in Texas. Her uncle was to meet her at the stagecoach office and take her to the ranch.

Cassie was afraid but she had no choice. She hugged her mother goodbye at the train station and got on the train. She had never been on one before and it was not proper for her to travel without an escort, but her father said no one would bother her.

She had been on the train for three days when there was an accident, and the train was derailed. She was thrown from her seat and hit her head. When she woke up people were rushing around and many women and children were crying. She sat up slowly and looked around at the chaos around her.

Her bag was gone and her purse with her money. She rose slowly and walked off the train. There were bodies lying everywhere on the ground around her. A man came to her and asked her if she was all right.

Cassie nodded.

He asked her what her name was, and she signed. He backed away from her and left.

Cassie saw a tree in the distance. She walked to it and sat on the ground watching everyone rush around.

She must have fallen asleep, because when she woke it was night and the bodies were gone. She looked around. Everyone was gone. No one noticed her sitting under the tree.

Cassie stood and walked to the train that was still on the tracks. She looked around and saw no one. She was alone. She went into one of the cars and saw a coat someone had left. Since the night was cool she put on the coat and looked around for anything to eat. She found the kitchen car and packed as much food as she could carry.

When she stepped off the train she looked around again and started walking down the tracks. There had to be a town up ahead somewhere.

Cassie walked all-night and stopped in the morning to eat. She spread her coat on the ground and lay down under a tree near the tracks. When she woke the sun was high in the sky. She ate some of the food she had taken, gathered up her coat and started following the tracks again.

She walked for two more days before she saw a station ahead. She hurried but found that there was only a station and one other building. There was a large water tank near the station. She had seen the train stop and take on water once.

She looked around and saw no one. It was near dark. She would have to wait until morning for someone to come. She lay down on the bench and covered herself with her coat and slept.

The next morning, she woke to find that there was no one at the station or the other building. She could not call out, so she ate some of her food and started walking down the tracks. She walked until mid afternoon before she saw someone. A man was riding on his horse beside the tracks. Cassie was afraid. He looked like he needed a bath, and his hair was longer than she had ever seen on a man.

Trevor heard someone behind him and pulled his gun from his holster as he turned his horse around.

Cassie stopped walking and stared at the gun the man had in his hand.

Trevor frowned at the woman on the tracks and lowered his gun. He kept his gun ready as he rode slowly towards her.

Cassie wanted to run but she kept looking at his gun and could not move.

Trevor stared at the woman. He looked around and saw no one else then back to her. "What are you doing out here alone?" When the woman did not say anything he said, "I'm not going to hurt you."

Cassie swallowed and put down her bag of food. She signed that her name was Cassie. She knew he would probably run away from her, but she had no choice.

Trevor put his gun away and stared at the woman moving her hands and frowned. "Can't you talk?"

Cassie shook her head. When she saw that he put his gun back into its holster, she picked up her bag of food and started walking past the man and his horse. She knew he would not help her.

Trevor watched the woman walk past him and down the tracks. He turned his horse and followed her.

Cassie walked down the tracks with Trevor following her for a long while before she stopped along the side of the tracks. She spread her coat out on the ground and sat down with her bag of food. She pulled out what food she had left and put it on the coat. She motioned for him to sit on the coat and held some of her food to him.

Trevor stared at the woman. She was offering him some of her food and from what he could see it was the last of it.

Trevor got off his horse and moved slowly towards her. He could see that she was afraid but did not move away.

Trevor sat on the coat and took the food she offered. She smiled at him and ate her food looking down the tracks. Trevor watched her as he ate. She was sure a strange one. Out here all alone. She should not be so trusting.

Cassie finished her meal and gathered her empty bag. She signed 'thank you' to the man and pulled on her coat. Trevor got up from her coat and watched her shake it out and put it back over her shoulders. She turned and started walking down the tracks.

Trevor shook his head. He had never seen anything like it. He walked back to his horse and mounted. He should just leave her, but he couldn't. He could offer her a ride but knew she would not accept it. She seemed to be content on walking down the tracks. Hell. He would have to ride along and see that she got to the next town safely. It would be two days before they reached the next town if they followed the tracks.

Trevor kicked his horse gently to get her moving and followed behind the woman as she walked down the tracks. He would have talked to her but did not know if she could hear him.

Cassie knew he was following her but did not stop. She was tired of walking and would like to ride but could not ask him. He seemed to be nice enough, but she did not know him, and he would not understand if she asked him for his name.

Cassie walked the rest of the day and stopped when it became dark. They had left the trees some time ago and the prairie stretched out in all directions. She looked around for a place to put her coat. She spread it on the ground and pulled part of it over her shoulders. The night had turned cold.

Trevor stopped his horse when she was on the ground and wrapped part of the coat around her. That was all? She was just going to sit there.

He knew the night was going to be cold. He sighed and got off his horse. He could at least build a fire and give her some of his food since she did share what she had left with him earlier.

Cassie watched the man gather sticks and start a fire. She put her hands towards the flames and smiled at him. Trevor shook his head at her and took some food from his saddlebags. He spread his bedroll on the ground near her and handed her some food.

Cassie signed 'thank you' and took the food.

Trevor watched her as she ate. She was a pretty thing when she smiled. Too bad she could not talk. Then again he smiled. A woman that could not talk. There had to be some good in that.

Cassie finished her meal and lay down on her coat. She was cold but at least she had something to eat.

Trevor saw her shaking and knew she was cold. That coat she had was not warm enough for the cold night. He built up the fire and took his coat and put it over her. She signed something again and pulled the coat up to her chin.

Trevor was beginning to understand that what she signed must have been 'thank you.' He tried to sign it back to her and she smiled and nodded.

He did not know why it made him feel so good when she smiled at him and did not want to think about it.

He lay on his bedroll and pulled his hat over his eyes. He would think about it more tomorrow.

When he woke the next morning, she was gone. He looked around and noticed that his horse, saddlebags, and everything were still there. He looked down the tracks and saw her far off in the distance. He gathered his bedroll and saddled his horse. By the time he caught up with her he was ready for his morning coffee and angry that she took off like that.

He pulled his horse to a stop in front of her to stop her. She looked up at him and waited. He dismounted and motioned for her to sit. She turned and walked away from the tracks and spread her coat on the ground and sat.

Trevor gathered more wood and built a fire. He sat on her coat next to her while his coffee brewed and handed her some jerky. It was not a great breakfast, but it would do.

Callie took the jerky and signed 'thank you' again. Trevor knew the sign now and nodded.

Since he had only one cup he let her have some coffee first. She drank only a little and offered him the cup. He drank the rest of it and poured some more and offered it to her. She drank more this time and handed him back the cup. Their fingers touched as he took back the cup and he felt the warmth of her fingers as they touched his. He almost jerked his hand back but grabbed the cup more firmly and drank deeply.

Trevor sat staring in the fire. He wished that she could at least hear him. He must have said it out loud because she touched his arm and nodded.

He frowned and said, "What?"

Cassie pointed to her ears and nodded.

Trevor looked at her ears and said, "You can hear me?"

Cassie nodded and smiled.

Trevor nodded back. "Okay then. There is no need for you to walk when you can ride with me. The way we are going now we will not reach the next town until two more days. If you ride with me we can be there by noon tomorrow."

Cassie looked at his horse and rose from the ground. She walked over and patted his horse's neck and turned to him and smiled. She signed that she would ride with him.

Trevor assumed that she said she would ride with him. He put out the fire, put his things back in the saddlebag and handed her the coat.

Cassie shook it out and put it on her shoulders. She waited until he mounted, and he put out his hand for her. She sat on the horse behind him and put her arms around his waist.

Trevor sat for a few minutes getting used to someone having their arms around him. He felt warm and tried to shake it off. They rode for a long way until Trevor stopped. He noticed the sky in the distance, and it looked like they were in for a thunderstorm. They only had a couple of hours before it would reach them.

He looked around and saw something in the distance that might be a line shack or some building they could use. "Those clouds do not look good." He pointed to what he saw in the distance. "That might be some shelter we can use."

He turned his horse and headed at a gallop towards the rise in the distance.

Cassie saw the clouds and held on as Trevor kicked his horse into a run for the shelter.

They did not make it before the rain began. They were lucky to find any shelter at all. The building was small, but it had a roof and a lean to for his horse.

Trevor took Cassie off the horse and led her to the door. He opened it and pushed her inside. He looked around and saw that it was a line shack that had been abandoned for some time. There was a bunk bed in the corner, a small stove for cooking and potbellied stove for warmth. "Can you start a fire?"

Cassie nodded.

"I'll put the horse in the lean to."

When Trevor left, Cassie removed her coat and hung it up on a peg by the door, then moved to the potbellied stove and started a fire.

There was some wood stacked between the stove and the potbellied stove. When the fire was started she looked in the cabinets in the small kitchen and found some canned goods and there was a locker with flour and coffee. She looked around and found some pans. She needed water. She looked out the window next to the stove. She saw a barrel of rainwater and smiled.

Trevor took his time unsaddling his horse and rubbing him down. He did not like that he liked Cassie having her arms around him as they rode. He would get her to the town as quickly as possible and leave. He was not in any hurry to get home, but he did not like how he felt when she was near.

When Trevor returned to the shelter it was still raining. He ran to the front door and entered closing the door behind him. He took off his hat and coat and put them on a peg next to the woman's coat. The room felt warm. He turned to say something to her, and his heart stopped.

The woman was standing by the table, in front of the stove, wearing nothing but a blanket. She had it wrapped around her under her arms and tied in front. Her shoulders were bare. Trevor tried to draw a breath but couldn't. Her skin was as white as snow and creamy looking.

Cassie looked up at him and smiled. She turned back to the biscuits she was making and did not notice the look on his face.

Trevor finally was able to draw a breath and looked at the potbelly stove. Anywhere but her. He saw her dress, stockings and under garments on a chair drying. Her shoes were on the floor next to the chair. All of a sudden it was too warm in the little shack. He needed to go back out into the cold rain and cool off. He turned to leave and felt her hand on his arm. He turned back to her and his heart stopped again.

Cassie smiled at him and motioned for him to come by the stove and warm up. She handed him a blanket and walked back to the table.

Trevor stood holding the blanket and did not know what to do next. He looked at the table and saw some cans and then to the stove. She had found a pot and had something cooking. He shook his head and moved to the potbelly stove and sat in the chair she had place there for him. He took off his boots and socks but remained dressed. There was no way he was going to take off his clothes.

Cassie touched his arm again some time later and motioned for him to come to the table. She picked up the chair he was sitting in and placed it across the table from hers.

Trevor moved towards the table and sat down. The woman knew how to cook. She placed a bowl of stew in front of him and biscuits. He tasted the stew and some of the biscuit and smiled at her. "This is good."

Cassie smiled and sat down to eat.

They ate in silence. When he was finished eating Trevor said, "I'm going to check on my horse." He knew it was a lame thing to say because he knew Buster was fine. But he had to get away from her.

Cassie nodded and started to clear the table.

Trevor stayed in the lean to with Buster for a long while before he returned to the shack. He held his breath as he entered. He hoped she was dressed.

Cassie's clothes had dried, and she put them back on. She was sitting in front of the potbelly stove when she heard Trevor return.

Trevor let out the breath he was holding when he saw that she was dressed. He moved to the stove to warm his hands.

Cassie wished she knew his name but there was nothing to write with to ask him. She looked at the wood next to the stove and had an idea.

She held the end of one of the sticks in the fire of the stove and put it into the ashes. She drew out the stick and wrote her name on the floor.

Trevor watched the woman and saw that she was writing something on the floor. He moved closer to her and saw that she wrote Cassie.

Trevor said, "Cassie."

Cassie nodded and pointed to him.

Trevor nodded and said, "Trevor."

Cassie smiled and signed his name.

Trevor noticed how long her fingers were and could feel them on his body. He turned away quickly and looked at the bunk beds. Thank God there was a place for them to sleep. If there had been one bed Trevor knew he would have slept on the floor.

Trevor did not sleep well knowing that Cassie was sleeping in the bunk below him. Below him. He almost groaned out load. The thought of her soft body beneath his kept him awake most of the night.

The rain did not stop all night. The next morning it was still raining. Trevor checked on his horse while Cassie made coffee and looked for something for them to eat. There were some canned goods left. She picked out a couple of cans and started the fire in the stove. They had some biscuits left from last night so when Trevor returned she had something ready for them to eat.

After breakfast Trevor noticed that the rain was easing up. "It looks like the rain might stop soon. If we ride hard we can be in the next town by dark."

Cassie nodded. She did not know what she would do when she arrived in the town, but she would think of something. She knew where the Circle T ranch was on a map but did not know where she was, but she would find out when she got there.

Since she had no money she hoped they had a telegraph office. She could wire her uncle and maybe he would send her money to get to the ranch.

Trevor and Cassie left at noon and rode as hard as they could with the ground so wet. They did not reach town until dusk. Trevor stopped in front of a hotel and helped Cassie down.

Cassie looked at the hotel and frowned. She had no money. She looked around and saw that there were some stables at the end of town. She turned to Trevor and signed 'thank you.'

Trevor nodded and took her arm to help her up the steps to the hotel. He stopped when she pulled her arm away.

Cassie shook her head at him and tried to sign that she had no money, but Trevor frowned at her. Cassie shook her head and turned and began walking towards the stables.

Trevor watched her walk away and frowned. He did not understand. He saw that she was walking towards the stables. Then it dawned on him. She had no money. She had nothing but her coat and an empty bag her food was in.

Trevor untied Busters reigns and followed her. When she reached the stables, she looked around. There was a young man in one of the stalls. She approached him and signed as best she could that she wanted to sleep in one of the stalls.

The young man looked at her. "If you want something ask for it."

Cassie tried to sign that she could not speak. The young man told her to go away and turned back to rubbing down a saddle.

Cassie sighed and turned to see Trevor behind her. She was embarrassed and looked away quickly. Cassie moved to go around him, but he put his hand on her arm to stop her and turned to the young man. "I need to stable my horse for the night."

The young man smiled and said, "Sure. I'll rub him down and see that he gets some oats. It'll be one dollar."

Trevor pulled a dollar from his pocket and handed it to the young man. The young man pointed to a stall and Trevor led his horse to it and held onto Cassie's arm. He told her to stay and removed his saddle and put his saddlebags over his shoulder. He took Cassie's arm and led her out of the stables.

"We are going to get something to eat and you are going to stay in the hotel."

Cassie tried to pull away, but Trevor tightened his grip. "Cassie you cannot stay in the stables or sleep outside somewhere. It is not safe."

Cassie nodded. She did not want him to spend his money on her but had no choice. Maybe her uncle would send enough money and she could pay him back.

Trevor entered the hotel and got a room. There was only one room left or he would have taken two. He took Cassie to the room. She sat in a chair by the bed and looked out the window.

Trevor put his saddlebags in the corner with his bedroll and said, "I'll sleep on the floor."

Cassie looked at the bed. It was big enough for two and shook her head.

Trevor frowned at her but said nothing. He was hungry and tired. He looked at the pitcher of water on the table next to the bed and said, "Let's get cleaned up and get some food."

Cassie nodded and poured some water into the basin and began to clean her face.

Trevor noticed her dress and how dirty it was and then looked at his own clothes. They both needed a bath. He would bring their food to the room and order them both a bath. "I'll get the food and order us a bath. I'll be right back."

Cassie looked at her dress and nodded. She had not noticed before how she must look to him. Her dress was dirty, and her hair felt dirty.

Trevor brought up their food and they ate in silence. When they were finished there was a knock on the door. He opened it and saw the hotel staff with a tub and buckets of water. He moved aside and let them enter.

Cassie looked at the tub and smiled and motioned for him to go first.

Trevor shook his head. "No this is for you. I'll go down to the barbershop. They have baths there."

Cassie nodded.

Trevor left with the hotel staff and did not want to think of all her lovely white, creamy body naked in the tub. Just seeing her shoulders was enough to make him groan.

Trevor took his time in the barbershop getting a haircut and bath. He passed a Mercantile that was just closing and thought of Cassie's dress. He stopped the man from closing and bought Cassie a new dress and other things that she would need.

Cassie did not want to put on her dirty dress. She put on her undergarments and wrapped herself in a blanket. She washed her dress and laid it over the chair to dry. She wished there were a fire to set it in front of.

She laid down on the bed and fell asleep.

Trevor opened the door slowly and looked in the room. Cassie was lying on the bed asleep wrapped in a blanket. He saw her dress on the chair and noticed that she tried to wash the dirt out. He was glad he purchased the dress and things for her.

Cassie opened her eyes when she heard Trevor enter the room. She sat up holding the blanket around her.

Trevor handed her a package and she frowned at him.

Trevor shrugged and said, "I bought you some things."

Cassie took the package and opened it. There was a new dress, a comb and bush for her hair, new undergarments, and stockings. She looked up at Trevor and signed 'thank you.'

Trevor nodded and moved away from the bed. He picked up his bedroll and spread it out on the floor.

Cassie did not say anything. If he wanted to sleep on the floor she would say nothing.

She put the package on the floor and climbed beneath the covers.

Trevor put out the light and lay on the floor on his bedroll and closed his eyes. He could smell the fragrance of roses and rolled away from her. It was a long time before he fell asleep.

The next morning Trevor rose early and left the room. He did not want to be there when Cassie woke and dressed.

When he came back an hour later she was dressed, and her hair was brushed. He had bought her a comb, so she could put up her hair if she wanted to. He closed the door to the room and stared at her. She was beautiful. Her hair was the color of the sun and the blue dress matched the blue in her eyes.

She smiled and turned around slowly.

Trevor took a deep breath. "Let's get some breakfast."

Cassie nodded and followed him down the stairs.

During breakfast Cassie was thinking of what to do. She would send a telegram to her uncle and wait for a reply. She wanted to talk to Trevor and tell him what happened on the train and let him know she had a place to go. There was some paper and a pen on a desk in the hotel lobby. After breakfast she would write it all down for him and say goodbye. She would find work in town somewhere until her uncle returned her telegram.

Trevor was thinking of what he would do next with Cassie. He did not know if she had a place to go and he could not stay here long. He had to get home. He had taken more time than he originally planned and there was a lot to be done when he got there.

He had sent his men home after the sale of the cattle. He stopped off to visit with his sister and brother-in-law for a while before heading home. But he needed to get back. If she did not have a place to go he could take her with him. He was only three days away from his ranch. "Cassie. I need to get back to my ranch. Do you have a place to go?"

Cassie nodded and she signed that she would write it out for him.

Trevor nodded.

Cassie stopped at the desk in the hotel lobby and wrote out her story for him while he waited. She handed him the paper and waited while he read it.

Trevor read the information and nodded. Her uncle, Josh Tremaine, owned the Circle T. He did not like the man. It was only a day's ride from his ranch. He could take her there. "The Circle T is only a day's ride from my ranch. I can take you there."

Cassie smiled and nodded. She liked Trevor and wanted to stay with him.

Trevor smiled and said, "Good. We can start in the morning. Let's see the town."

Cassie nodded and took his arm. They spent the morning walking around town. She sent a telegram to her uncle saying she would be there in a few days.

When they returned to the hotel there was note for Trevor. He read the note and frowned. Cassie put a hand on his arm, and he looked at her. He did not say anything but put his hand over hers on his arm and turned to go up the stairs.

When they were in the room he handed Cassie the letter. He told his father that he would be staying at the hotel before he returned to the ranch.

Cassie read the note and hugged Trevor. His father had died while he was away. Trevor put his arms around her and buried his face in her hair. It had been just him and his father for a long time.

Trevor kissed her hair and lifted her chin to kiss her lips softly. He needed someone right now and he had wanted her since that first day he had seen her.

Cassie had never been kissed before, but she liked it. She parted her lips to tell him and Trevor took her lips again in a hard kiss. Cassie was surprised at the warmth that she felt but soon relaxed and kissed him back.

Trevor ran his hands over her back and pulled her closer when he felt her response. He knew this was wrong, but he needed someone right now. He needed her.

Cassie did not pull away as his hands moved to her breast. She knew he needed someone right now and the thought of him wanting her excited her.

Trevor ended the kiss and put her head on his chest holding her there as his hands gently caressed her. "Cassie." He whispered. "I need you."

Cassie raised her head and smiled. She rose up and kissed his lips softly and led him to the bed.

He lay down with her and pulled her into his arms. He kissed her for a long while running his hands over her before he unbuttoned her dress and kissed her neck. Cassie sighed and kissed his hair and held on to him.

The afternoon passed without their knowledge. They were in their own world discovering each other and loving.

Trevor made love to Cassie twice before he pulled her to him and slept. When he awoke later he thought about what he had done and sighed. He had loved his father and he needed someone. She came to him so willingly that he could not turn away from what she offered.

Cassie came awake and found Trevor staring at her. They were still naked under the covers and she felt his warm body next to hers. She smiled at him and kissed him.

Trevor was going to apologize to her but when she kissed him, he kissed her back and could think of nothing but to be inside her again.

Cassie put her head on his shoulder and sighed. This was the only time she would feel like this. She knew he would take her to her uncle and ride away. No one wanted her because she could not speak. She closed her eyes and breathed in the smell of him and ran her hands over his nipple and down his ribs to his waist. She felt and heard his sharp intake of breath as her hand roamed lower. She smiled and took him in her hand.

Trevor was in heaven and hell. He took her hand and showed her how to please him. He stopped breathing as Cassie started kissing his chest and trailed kisses down his ribs to his stomach and kept going. He moaned when she kissed him where her hand was, and his hips came off the bed when she took him in her mouth.

Cassie wanted to know what he tasted like. He had tasted her. She smiled. He tasted good. She returned her mouth to him and licked him and ran her tongue over him. She liked the way he moaned and lifted his hips off the bed as she kissed him and ran her tongue over him.

Trevor could stand it no more and grabbed Cassie's shoulders and moved back on the bed so that he could roll on top of her. He entered her quickly and set the pace. He had lost all control and was almost brutal in his taking of her.

Cassie matched his pace and when she climaxed she thought she would die. The pleasure was so intense. Trevor felt her climax and ended the kiss when he followed her into a world that was only theirs.

Trevor lay on top of her breathing hard. He moved to his side and pulled her with him. They lay there holding each other for a long while before their breathing returned to normal.

They dressed and went down to dinner but returned to the room and made love all night.

In the morning Trevor held Cassie in his arms and knew he had to say something about yesterday and last night, but he did not know what to say.

Cassie woke and kissed Trevor gently on the lips before she got out of bed and dressed for the day. She knew that their time was over. She could see the regret in Trevor's eyes. He needed someone and she was near. That was all there was. She would miss him and remember their time together for always.

Trevor watched her get dressed and said nothing.

After breakfast they saddled Buster and rode out of town. For the next two days he said nothing to her and slept in his own bedroll at night. He would be glad to be rid of her. She was not what he needed right now. With his father gone there would be a lot more to do around the ranch.

When they arrived at the Circle T ranch her uncle, Josh Tremaine, was waiting on the porch for her. "Bout time you got here." Was all he said.

Trevor helped her down from the horse. He did not like the way the man talked to her but said nothing.

The man walked down the steps but did not look like he was please to see her. "Get to the kitchen and get busy. You were supposed to be here days ago."

Cassie nodded and turned to Trevor. She signed 'thank you.'

Josh took her by the arm and roughly pushed her towards the house. "I'll have none of that. Now get in the house."

Trevor moved forward but Josh stopped him. "Thanks for bringing her to me Danvers. I hope she was no trouble. Sorry to hear about your father."

Trevor nodded but did not take his eyes off of Cassie as she walked up the steps and into the house. "No. She was no trouble." Trevor knew he had to get home but did not want to leave Cassie here. It was none of his affair and he needed to get home.

Trevor mounted quickly and rode towards home.

Cassie heard him ride away as she walked down the hall to the kitchen. A tear fell from her eye and she wiped it away. When she found the kitchen, she looked around and saw that no one had been there to clean it for a long while. She put her bag, with her things in it, near the door and started to work.

Trevor was busy the next few weeks on the ranch. With his father gone there was lot to do. One day he was riding fence and came across some of Tremaine's men moving some cattle. He nodded to them over the fence and continued on his way. He had been thinking of Cassie often, especially at night. He had lost a lot of sleep thinking about the way she had made love to him in the hotel.

A month after he had left her at the Circle T he found a reason to visit. Some of his cattle had come up missing and there was a break in the fence between his ranch and the Circle T.

Trevor rode out early in the morning and arrived at the Circle T at noon. Josh Tremaine was sitting in a chair on the front porch when he rode up. He nodded to Trevor and asked, "Danvers. What brings you here."

Trevor dismounted and walked up the steps. "Some of my cattle are missing. There is a break in the fence in the north pasture."

Josh stood and motioned for Trevor to follow him into the house. Trevor wanted to see Cassie but tried not to look around as he followed Josh into the study.

Josh sat behind his desk and motioned for Trevor to sit in the chair. He offered Trevor a cigar. When Trevor shook his head, he lit one and asked. "I'll have my foreman look for your cattle. How is it going without your father?"

Trevor knew where this was heading. Josh had been trying to buy their ranch for years. His father would not sell and now that he was gone, he knew that the extra work might change Trevor's mind. Josh never did think that some one as young as Trevor could run the ranch by himself. But he did not know that Trevor had been running the ranch practically on his own for the past two years since his father became ill.

"Fine. How is it going here?"

Josh shrugged. "Good as usual." He stared at Trevor then said, "You know my offer to buy your spread still stands."

Trevor nodded and stood. "No thanks Mr. Tremaine."

Josh rose as Trevor stood. He was going to say something but saw that Cassie was standing in the doorway of the study. He frowned and asked harshly "What do you want?"

Trevor turned to see who Josh was talking to so harshly and saw Cassie. He smiled but lost it quickly when he saw her. She looked well but the life in her eyes that was always there was gone.

Cassie smiled at him and was going to sign something but looked at her uncle and quickly dropped her hands. She took a card from her pocket and held it up. It read 'lunch.'

Josh nodded and motioned for her to leave.

Cassie looked at Trevor once more and returned to the kitchen.

Trevor was angry. Tremaine was treating her like a simpleton.

Josh did not notice Trevor was angry and asked, "Would you stay and have something to eat before you ride out?"

Trevor thought to say no but he wanted to see Cassie again, so he nodded.

Josh smiled and led the way to the dining room. They sat at the table and Cassie appeared carrying food for the table. Josh said, "Bring another plate."

Cassie stared at Trevor for only a moment before she left to get him a plate. She set his plate in front of him and served her uncle's food and turned to serve Trevor.

Trevor did not like that she was treated like this and held up his hand. "I'll serve myself."

Cassie nodded and left.

Trevor had a hard time eating and wanted to do nothing more than leave as quickly as possible.

Cassie stood in the kitchen and did not see anything for the tears in her eyes. She did not want Trevor to see her like this. It was so good to see him. He looked well. She laughed to herself. He looked wonderful.

She wiped her eyes and began cleaning up. The door to the dining room opened and she turned quickly to see what her uncle wanted and saw Trevor standing in the doorway. She tried to smile then noticed he was holding his plate in his hands. She rushed to him and took the plate. If her uncle saw him helping her he would punish her.

Cassie put the plate on the kitchen table and signed 'thank you.' She did not notice her uncle standing behind Trevor.

Josh pushed Trevor aside when he saw Cassie sign with her hands and rushed to her and slapped her. "I said none of that in my house you stupid creature."

Trevor could stand it no more. He pushed Tremaine aside and pulled Cassie along with him as he rushed out of the house.

Tremaine followed. "What do you think you are doing?"

Trevor put Cassie on his horse. "I am taking her with me." He turned to Tremaine and said, "If you ever hit her again, I'll kill you."

Trevor mounted and rode out of the yard. He did not stop until he was back on his own land. He pulled up near a stand of trees and helped Cassie down from the horse. "I'm sorry Cassie, but when he hit you…"

Cassie put her hand on his arm and smiled at him.

Trevor could not stand being so close to her without kissing her. He pulled her into his arms and kissed her. He was so hungry for her that he crushed her to him in a hold he knew was too strong.

Cassie did not notice that he was crushing her to him. She only felt his kiss and kissed him with all the love she had for him.

When Trevor raised his head, he knew he was holding her too tight and loosened his hold. He laid her head on his chest and stroked her hair. He was quiet for a long time and then he realized that he loved her. He wanted to love her every night and wake up each morning with her nearby. "Cassie. Will you marry me?"

Cassie raised her head and frowned at him. She loved him but he would be sorry later. Her uncle grew angrier every day that she was there. She could not stand it if Trevor felt like that.

Trevor knew what she was thinking. Because she could not speak she did not think anyone would want her. "Cassie. It does not matter to me that you cannot speak. I love you just the way you are."

Cassie smiled and kissed him.

Trevor kissed her back and remembered this time not to hold her so tight.

Love Cannot Be Denied

"True love cannot be found where it does not exist, nor can it be denied where it does."
Torquato Tasso

To Everyone that believes in Love and for those that need more convincing.

"I have come to see General Raymond."

"Do you have an appointment ma'am."

"No, I do not."

Lieutenant Russell shook his head. "I am sorry ma'am the General is very busy. I can make an appointment for you for next week."

"No thank you, today will be fine."

"I am sorry ma'am; I can't let you see him today."

"Really." Ruth moved around the Lt.'s desk and headed for the General's door.

"I am sorry ma'am, but you cannot go in there." Lt. Russell said trailing after Ruth.

Ruth did not stop. She reached the General's door, opened it, and walk into his office.

General Jonathan Raymond was looking through some papers on his desk when his door opened. He looked up and saw a woman walk into his office trailed by his Lieutenant.

Lt. Russell said, "I am sorry sir. I told her she had to make an appointment, but she just walked in."

General Raymond looked at the woman. "I am sorry ma'am, but I am very busy right now. If you will excuse me." He looked at the papers on his desk dismissing both her and his Lieutenant.

Lt. Russell took her arm to escort her out of the General's office, but she would not move. "I think not. I will have a word with you General. Now."

General Raymond stood and looked at Lt. Russell. "Remove this woman from my office Lieutenant. Now."

"Yes sir." He turned to Ruth and said, "Ma'am please let me escort you outside and we can make you an appointment."

Ruth held her ground and looked at the Lieutenant. "No." then she looked at the General and said, "You serve this country. I am a citizen of this country. My tax dollars pay your salary. I will speak with you now."

General Raymond stared at the woman and she stared right back. He could see that he could not intimidate her. He did not want to make a scene and this woman would do it. Jon sighed and said, "Very well, but only a few minutes."

Then he turned to Lt. Russell and said, "We will speak later. Dismissed."

Lt. Russell saluted him and left closing the door behind him.

Jon motioned for the woman to sit down. When she did he sat in his chair and said, "Now ma'am how I can help you?"

"My son is being accused of espionage. I want the charges dropped."

This was not what he expected. "I am afraid I cannot do that ma'am. There is evidence against him."

"It is false. He is being framed. I do not like your politics General. I will not have my son be a scapegoat. I want the person responsible caught and my son released. You have three weeks to release him."

Jon looked at the woman hard. Was she threatening him? "I am sorry, but I did not get your name."

"Ms. Ruth Cummings"

Cummings. Now why does that name sound familiar? Jon reached in his bottom drawer and pulled out a book he had been reading. He looked at the back cover. Written by Ruth Cummings.

He looked at her and said, "Exactly what will happen in three weeks Ms. Cummings?"

Ruth rose from her chair and said, "My look at the time. I have taken enough of yours."

When Ruth turned to leave Jon said, "Are you threatening me Ms. Cummings?"

Ruth did not answer until she reached the door. She opened it and looked back at General Raymond. "Certainly not General. It was a promise."

Ruth walked out of his office and closed the door. She turned to the Lt. "Thank you Lieutenant you were most helpful."

Lt. Russell stared at her back as she left. The General buzzed him, and he went into his office.

General Raymond was pacing back and forth when Lt. Russell appeared.

"General."

Jon did not stop his pacing. "Lieutenant find out what you can about Ms. Ruth Cummings. I want it on my desk first thing tomorrow morning."

"Yes, sir"

After the Lieutenant left Jon made a phone call. "We may have just received what we have been waiting for. I had a visitor today. One Ms. Ruth Cummings. Why didn't I know that the young officer charged with espionage was her son?"

"Sorry sir. We didn't think it was relevant."

Jon said in an angry tone. "Not relevant? My God man, don't you read? That woman is ruthless. She knows more about what goes on in Washington then the President."

"Um.. sorry sir."

Jon sighed. "You just make sure nothing happens to Lt. Randall. If one hair of his head is out of place you will pay for it." Jon hung up the phone and looked at the book he had been reading written by Ruth Cummings. He slammed it down on his desk and said, "Damn."

Ruth went to see her son. She was told she could not see him. She smiled at the officer and handed him a letter. When he saw who it was from he stood at attention and said, "Yes, ma'am."

Jason looked up and saw his mother standing at his cell door. He shook his head and walked to the bars. "Mother."

Ruth nodded and looked at the officer standing next to her. "Go away. Now." The young officer nodded and hurried away.

Jason smiled. "Mother you cannot order officers around."

"Why not?"

Jason sighed and said, "Never mind."

"How are you Jason. Are they treating you well?"

"Yes, Mother. I get three meals a day."

"I went to see General Raymond today."

Jason was not surprised but it still angered him. "Mother stay out of this. You don't know what is involved. These men are dangerous. I got too close."

Ruth looked around and smiled. She knew they were being monitored. "Well actually I know who they are. I have written a book about them that will be released in three weeks. If anything happens to you I will put actual names in it."

Jason knew what she was doing. She knew that everything they said was being heard. "Mother you do not. Don't make rash threats."

Ruth looked at her son and said, "Hmm."

"What is that supposed to mean?"

"Jason I will do whatever I have to, to get you out of here and if that means exposing the people behind your being here then so be it. It was their mistake after all. They did not even have the intelligence to find out that you were my son. How stupid can anyone be?"

Jason sighed. He knew there was no stopping her. He also knew that if anyone can get him out of her it would be her. So, Jason said what his brother and sister always said, "Yes Mother."

Ruth nodded and said, "I will see you in a few days. I have some errands to run. I will send over some of your favorite books."

"Mother they won't let you bring anything with you nor can I receive any packages."

"We will see."

The next morning three of his favorite books were delivered to him by noon. Jason just shook his head. He felt sorry for the bad guys.

Ruth was worried. It was true that she had a new book being released in three weeks, but it did not have anything to do with this mess. She hoped they would take the bait and make a move. She was sending Jason messages in his books. She hoped he picked up on them. She deliberately made visits to important people today in hopes of making them think she had information.

Ruth was making dinner when her doorbell rang. She wiped her hands on the dishtowel and opened the door.

General Raymond stood at her door. "Don't you check to see who is at your door before you open it? I could have been anyone."

Ruth smiled and said, "If you weren't anyone I was expecting you would not have gotten this far. Won't you come in?"

Jon nodded and entered her apartment.

Ruth closed the door and said, "I was just fixing some dinner would you like to stay?"

Jon skipped lunch and he as hungry. "Thank you, but you might not want me to stay after you hear what I have come to say."

Ruth smiled and said, "Nonsense. Come into the kitchen and you can help me."

Jon followed her into the kitchen. Ruth pulled an apron from a drawer and tied it around his waist. Jon looked down at the apron and back to Ruth.

Ruth smiled and said, "Just in case."

Ruth went to the refrigerator and took out vegetables for the salad. She put them on the counter, pulled a knife from a drawer and a bowl from the cupboard.

"You can make the salad." The she turned to him and said, "You can make a salad can't you?"

"Of course, I can make a salad."

Ruth nodded and started cutting up chicken for the casserole she was making.

They worked in silence. Jon was cutting up the vegetables for the salad and Ruth made the casserole.

When Ruth was done she put the casserole in the oven and stood by Jon. He was very good at chopping up vegetables.

She folded her arms and leaned against the counter watching him. "You are very good at that."

Jon shrugged and said, "I have lived alone for a long time. It helps if you learn how to cook. Eating out all the time loses its appeal after a while."

Ruth nodded. "Yes, it does."

Jon stopped cutting up vegetables and said, "Ms. Cummings."

Ruth stopped him by saying, "Ruth. I think fixing dinner together calls for first names."

Jon looked at her said, "Jon."

Ruth nodded and went into the living room to put on some music. "Jon what kind of music do you like?"

Jon shrugged. "Most any kind. I like soft Jazz best though."

"So do I."

Ruth put in a CD of soft Jazz then went back into the kitchen to pull a bottle of wine from the refrigerator. She poured two glasses and handed one to Jon.

He had finished the salad.

She put it in the refrigerator.

"Let's sit in the living room. The casserole should be done in about 45 minutes."

Jon took off his apron and followed her out of the kitchen.

Ruth sat at one end of the couch and Jon sat on the other. Ruth smiled at him as she took a sip of wine. He was nervous. Interesting.

They sat in silence for a minute or two listening to the music before Jon said, "Ruth the reason I am here…"

She cut him off saying. "After dinner. Tell me about yourself."

Jon shrugged. "Not much to tell. Joined the Army young and made a career of it."

"Wife, children?" Ruth asked.

"Married once, didn't work out. No children."

"Favorite color."

"Blue."

"Favorite sport"

"Football."

"Favorite pastime."

"Going fishing."

Then Jon said, "Husband? Boyfriend? Children?"

Ruth smiled. "Once didn't work out, none, and three."

"Favorite color."

"Blue."

"Favorite sport."

"Baseball."

"Favorite pastime."

"People."

Jon said, "Your favorite pastime is people?"

"Yes, I find people interesting. There are little things about them that gives themselves away. Usually, it only takes me a few minutes to determine a person's true character."

Jon wanted to ask her what she thought his true character was but wasn't sure he wanted to know. He had better change the subject. "What made you start writing?"

"Had to. I saw a panel of writers one-day on a talk show. A member of the audience asked them why they write. They said, *because they have to. A story comes into their head and they have to write it down in order for it to go away.* Then I realized that is what happens to me."

"You write a lot about the military and politics. Why?"

Ruth shrugged. "It's easy. If you understand people you know what they are capable of. People don't change, situations do. If you understand a person's character you know what they are going to do. How they are going to react to a situation."

Jon shook his head. "That is like reading a person's mind. You can't know how a person will react in every situation."

Ruth shrugged and said, "I am not surprised often."

"So why the military and politics?

"Because it is easy. There is always intrigue and mystery."

"What do you mean? How is there intrigue and mystery?"

"How many of my books have you read?"

Jon shrugged. "Quite a few."

"Was any of them unbelievable? Too farfetched. Way out there?"

"No. That's what makes it scary. They were believable. You made the characters so real. It seems that you would have a lot of enemies with what you write about?"

"Why?"

"Because your books always find the bad guy a military officer or a politician."

"Yes, but how many good military officers and politicians do I talk about?"

Jon shrugged. "I don't know. I don't think about them."

"There are a lot of military officers and politicians that believe in their country and its people. Read one of my books again and you will find that the few do not outweigh the many. In fact, I know a lot of secrets on a lot of people, but I do not write about them nor do I expose them."

"Oh, like what?"

Ruth laughed and said, "Oh no. They would not be secrets if I told."

"Don't you think it is dangerous knowing secrets about people?"

Ruth shook her head. "No. They all know that I would never indulge any information to anyone."

"How do they know that?"

"Because they know they can trust me."

Jon was going to ask how people knew she could be trusted when the buzzer went off in the kitchen.

Ruth stood and said, "Dinner. You get the salad and I'll set the table."

Ruth got the casserole out of the oven, set the table, and poured more wine. Jon put the salad on the table and sat down.

They discussed movies, books, and fun times over dinner.

When dinner was over Jon helped Ruth clean up the kitchen and took their wineglasses into the living room. Ruth put in another CD and sat on the couch.

Jon sat on the couch but not as far away from her this time and Ruth smiled as she took a sip of wine.

Jon was quiet for a minute then asked. "Why do people trust you?"

Ruth smiled and said, "Because I am trustworthy."

Jon stared at her until she said, "Because I cannot be bought. I have no love of money or material things. Those who would sell out their country or make political deals always do them for monetary gain or power. I don't covet either."

Jon looked at his wineglass and asked, "What did you hope to gain when you came into my office?"

"Oh, was there something to gain?"

Jon looked at her and said, "That's what I would like to know."

Ruth shrugged. "I just made a visit to your office. What do you think I hoped to gain?"

"Your son's release."

Ruth shrugged and did not make a comment.

Jon sighed. "Ruth, you threatened to expose information that could be dangerous. That puts you in danger. You were heard talking to your son about it yesterday. Do you really think you are invincible? That someone will not attempt to get the information you think you have?"

"You were eavesdropping on a private conversation? Shame on you."

Jon was getting angry she was not taking this situation serious. She put herself in danger. Anyone could have overheard the conversation. "Damn it, Ruth. This is not a joke. Lives are at stake. Your life is at stake here."

Ruth sighed and said, "Jon I am taking this very seriously. I appreciate your concern."

Ruth paused and said, "Actually you are in more danger than me."

Jon was surprised and raised an eyebrow at her. "Why do you say that?"

"Because you are one of the good guys."

She surprised him again. "What makes you think so?"

Ruth shrugged and did not answer.

Jon said in a dangerous tone, "Ruth."

Ruth sighed and said, "Because you wore the apron, fixed the salad, you like Jazz, had dinner with me, you like to go fishing, because you would rather fix a meal at home then eat out and you haven't made a pass at me."

"What the hell has that got to do with anything?"

"Because you are real. You have a kind, compassionate nature, your understanding, patient, caring, you finish what you start, you enjoy challenges and get bored easily." She smiled and said, "Enough?"

Jon did not speak for a long time. He looked at the wine in his glass and took a sip. "Where does 'because I haven't made a pass at you' fit in?"

"It doesn't."

Jon looked at her and asked, "Then why did you mention it?"

Ruth shrugged and stood. "Would you like some more wine?"

Jon nodded and gave her his wineglass.

Jon was looking over her music selection when she returned. She walked over to him and handed him his glass of wine.

Jon selected a CD and put it on to play. He took her wineglass from her and set both glasses on the table. The music played softly in the background as he took her in is arms and began to dance with her.

Ruth laid her head on his shoulder as they moved to the music. The longer they dance the more she could feel him. He was a warm and compassionate man. She had been alone for a long time. Maybe he would be her friend.

Jon had been alone a long time. He had never met anyone like Ruth. He liked the warmth he felt while holding her. She was fun to be with, intelligent and sexy as hell.

He put his hand under her chin and raised her face to look at his and said, "Ruth, this is not a good idea."

Ruth smiled and said, "I know." Then she kissed him gently on the lips. When she pulled away he tightened his hold on her and kissed her gently. When he felt her response, he kissed her harder.

He had never felt like this before. The floor could open up and he wouldn't care as long as she was with him.

Ruth was glad he was holding her because she wasn't sure she could stand on her own.

They danced and kissed moving to the music. They did not know when one song ended, and another began. They only knew each other. When the CD had finally run out of songs Jon stopped. He kissed Ruth one more time and said, "I'd better go."

Ruth said, "No. Don't go."

Jon pulled her to him again. Kissed her once more and said, "Ruth.." He did not finish what he was going to say, because she took his hand and led him towards her bedroom.

He stopped at the door and said, "You are sure I am one of the good guys?"

Ruth said, "I'll let you know in the morning."

Jon laughed. Picked her up, laid her on the bed and followed her down. He undressed her while she undressed him.

Ruth had never had such a climax. She just knew that with Jon it would be different, and it was.

Jon had never been caressed and loved like Ruth loved him all night. They made love three times and it wasn't enough.

Jon woke in the morning with Ruth's head on his shoulder and her arm across his waist. He kissed her hair and ran his hand down her arm, over her buttocks and up her back. She sighed and snuggled closer to him.

"Ruth I have to get up."

Ruth smiled and said, "You sure are frisky for an old General but let me check." Ruth moved her hand down to caress him and he groaned.

"Ruth you are going to kill me."

"Yeah, but what a way to go."

They made love again. They took a shower and Ruth fixed him breakfast.

After breakfast he said, "Ruth I want to know if you really have evidence about the espionage, your son is being accused of. You could be in danger and need protection."

"Jon I have protection. I have some errands to run today. Since it is Friday would you like to go to my cabin for the weekend? There is a great lake for fishing nearby. We could leave tonight. It's only a two-hour drive."

"What protection and what errands?"

Ruth sighed. "Jon are you going to come with me this weekend or not?"

Stubborn woman, Jon thought.

Stubborn man, Ruth thought.

Both Ruth and Jon spoke at the same time.

"Ruth"

"Jon"

Jon shook his head. Why did he think he could win against Ruth? "Ruth let's compromise. Either tell me about this protection of yours or what errands you have to make. Indulge me. I care about you and want to make sure you are not in danger."

Ruth nodded and said, "I have been thinking about the case against Jason, my son. I think I know where I can get some information. I have some favors to collect on and I am going to see them today."

"No. You are to stay out of this. If anyone even thinks you know something, they will kill you. I can't believe your son would allow you to be involved."

"My son knows I can take care of myself. Now what are you going to do today?"

"Follow you around to keep you safe."

Ruth shook her head. "I don't think so. You will scare everyone away."

"What do you mean?"

"Jon you can be very intimidating when you want to be, but I prefer to use sugar and spice to get the information I want. Not threaten to tie them to the rack."

"Sugar and spice." Jon sighed. He never thought that maybe last night was a usual occurrence for her that maybe it did not mean as much to her as did him.

Ruth knew what he was thinking. She only meant she would be nice not threatening and they did not talk about last night.

"Jon. I haven't been with a man in five years and never in my life have I experienced anything like last night. When I say sugar and spice it simply means I will be nice not threatening. I ask questions in a roundabout way to get the information I need. Not direct ones. No one suspects what I am really asking because they don't know people like I do."

Jon stared at her for a moment then pulled her out of her chair and kissed her. "Last night was the first time for me in a long time also and I never felt like that in my life. I just want you to be safe."

"I will be. I promise. I know what I am doing. Trust me."

Jon smiled at her and kissed her again.

"Now how about this weekend? I hope to have a lot to tell you."

Jon nodded and kissed her again before he left.

Ruth got dressed and went on her errands. Jon was going to meet her at her apartment at 6 pm. She stopped for lunch at her favorite restaurant. She took her usual booth in the corner and was soon joined by two men.

Ruth smiled at them. "Brady, Rosco what a pleasant surprise. What time?"

"Now."

Ruth sighed and said, "I hope I get lunch." Ruth picked up her purse and followed the men out the back door of the restaurant.

Ruth did not get back to her apartment until 5:45. She had just enough time to change into her jeans and T-shirt before Jon arrived. She had found out some interesting things today.

Jon arrived at 6 pm and knocked on her door. He was not in uniform like he was the night before. Before he could knock again four men surrounded him. One held a gun on him. They pushed him up against the wall and one man searched him. When he was through he turned him around and told Jon to put his hands on his head.

Ruth heard the knock and opened her door to find Brady, Rosco, Brain and Keith standing in the hallway with Jon. She looked at Jon then back to Brady.

"Um. Brady this is General Raymond. He was here last night. We are going to my cabin for the weekend. We have some business to discuss."

Brady nodded and said, "Your cabin is secure." Then he turned to Jon and said, "Sorry General. We did not recognize you out of uniform."

Ruth took Jon's arm and pulled him into her apartment. She knew he was going to question her, but she hoped it could wait until they got to the cabin.

He did not wait.

"What was that all about?"

"Jon, let's talk about it at the cabin."

Jon folded his arms across his chest and stared at her.

Ruth walked up to him put her arms around his neck and nibbled on his lips until he wrapped his arms around her and kissed her hard.

He did not release her for a long time. When he did he sighed and said, "Let's go."

Ruth smiled and got her bag out of the bedroom.

Jon did not know what to expect but if she thought this was a cabin then he would hate to see what she considered a mansion.

Jon looked around and followed Ruth into the bedroom. She took him on a tour of the cabin.

The cabin was a three-bedroom house. There was a porch around the entire building, a Jacuzzi, and a sauna. One bedroom was downstairs and a family room apart from the living room. There was a study with every piece of electronic equipment imaginable, and two bedrooms upstairs.

The living room had a large couch and two chairs facing the fireplace. There was a large rug on the floor between the fireplace and the couch.

They had stopped for dinner on the way, but Jon was curious what was in the refrigerator. He opened the door to the refrigerator and found it fully stocked. He opened the freezer and found steaks, fish, poultry, vegetables, and ice cream. There were two pies on the counter.

Jon looked through the cupboards. Pulled two bowls down, cut two pieces of pie and put ice cream on both.

Ruth was in the bedroom putting away the clothes she brought.

Jon called to her to come and get dessert.

She appeared in the kitchen and smiled. They ate their dessert and Jon took her into the living room and sat her on the couch.

He kissed her gently. Put her on one end of the couch and sat at the other. Ruth raised an eyebrow at him.

"You stay over there. I want some answers."

Ruth knew what he wanted. "Okay you ask, and I will answer the ones I can."

Jon did not like that but at least it was something.

"Who were those men outside your door."

"My protection."

Jon sighed. It was going to be a long weekend.

"Your errands today. Did you find out anything?"

"Yes. Quite a bit actually."

"I went by to see my son. He had a lot of information for me. It seems that there is a new type of satellite that is due to launch next month. It is supposed to be used only for monitoring the weather. It seems that it is going to be used for more than that. It has the capability of capturing not only information from other satellites but also can capture information from wireless transmissions. This information of course if going to a foreign government. The problem is that no one knows who is behind it. But I think I found the answer today."

"If your son gave you any information then it is common knowledge by now. All conversations are taped, and all visits are monitored on a camera. Anything he passes to you can be confiscated and anything you say is recorded."

"Hmm. Yes. Be that as it may. Believe what I am saying is true. Meanwhile there is a subcommittee looking into satellite's being used as possible weapons. Spy on the spy concept. Anyway. It will not be easy getting the information we need. I have an appointment on Monday that should give us what we need. It will be tricky, but I think I can do it."

"What subcommittee. When was it formed?

"It is a hush, hush one and it was formed last year."

"How do you know about it?"

"I am on it."

Jon stared at Ruth for a long while before he said, "What is this 'we' business. You were supposed to stay out of this."

"'We' means you and me. I got the okay today to ask you to help me."

"Okay from whom?"

"Sorry, can't tell you."

Jon stared at her and said, "You know maybe I should ask you for protection."

"Don't worry about that. You were protected this afternoon as soon as I got the okay."

Jon shook his head then looked at Ruth. His eyes travel over her. Her eyes, nose mouth, chin, neck, breasts, waist and then back up. "mmmm.. It's getting late." He rose from the couch and offered her his hand. She smiled and placed her hand in his.

They made love until early morning. It was almost noon before they had breakfast. After breakfast they walked down to the lake and while Jon was fishing Ruth sat on the bank and watched.

For dinner they fixed the fish Jon caught. After dinner they sat on the couch and talked, they danced to soft music and made love on the rug.

Sunday morning when Ruth woke she did not linger in bed. She kissed Jon and said, "We are meeting someone today. Get dressed. I'll fix breakfast. We have about an hour drive ahead of us."

"Who are we going to meet?"

"Someone."

Jon sighed and went to shower. She can be so stubborn. Then Jon stopped and thought of something else that she was, trustworthy. Of all his years in the military he had never done so many things without being in command of them or knowing what was going on. He never followed anyone blindly, but here he was following her around.

Jon shook his head in wonder.

Ruth did not fill Jon in until they got to the meeting place.

"We are meeting Senator Reinhardt. He is the head of the subcommittee. It seems that when this subcommittee started we were to keep it to ourselves but there has been a leak. The information that has been gathered is top secret. Anyone can take that information and produce exactly what is being produced with the weather satellite. When we found out about the satellite we knew that information was being sold. Senator Reinhardt has some information that may help us find who is behind this."

"You said you had an idea of who is behind it. Who do you suspect?"

"You."

Jon looked at her in surprise. "What? Are you crazy? You think I would sell out my country?"

"No. The information is coming from your office. I suspected you at first. That is why I went to see you. To get your measure. Then when you showed up at my apartment..."

Jon did not let her finish. Jon was angry. She used him. What they shared meant nothing to her. "You used me. This was all part of the plan to free your son. You brought me up here to try and get information from me. Damn you Ruth." Jon walked away from her. He walked past the car and followed the road that would lead him to a small town. He could make a phone call and get back on his own. Damn her. None of what they shared meant anything to her. Everything she said was a lie.

Jon was a quarter mile down the road when he heard the gun shot. He turned quickly and ran back to Ruth. She had to be all right.

Jon veered off the road and approached the meeting place through the forest. He looked around as he moved slowly towards the meeting place. He moved so he could see where he left Ruth standing. His heart stopped.

She was lying on the ground where he had left her. He wanted to rush to her but had to be careful. If she was still alive he had to get her out of there. He had to make sure the area was secure first. And where was her damn protection.

Jon circled the area staying hidden in the trees. He could do nothing until he knew no one was around. The only evidence that there was anyone there was Ruth lying in the dirt. He did not have a weapon on him so he was limited in what he could do if he came across someone with a gun.

Jon watched and listened. Nothing. He made his way towards her. He crouched low and was going from tree to tree. He had to pull her to the tree just to the left of where she is lying. Out in the open like she was, made her an easy target. He would also be an easy target if he tried to get to her.

Jon moved quickly to her side and dragged her behind the tree. She was breathing. There was too much blood to see how badly she was wounded. He had to get her back to the little town and hoped to God they had a doctor.

Jon put Ruth over his shoulder and ran for the car. He opened the driver's door and a bullet hit the door. He pushed her inside and followed her. There were three more shots that rang out hitting the car as he started the engine and backed the car down the road.

One bullet grazed his arm, but he did not feel it. He had to get Ruth to a doctor. He saw a place in the road where he could turn the car around. It took precious minutes, but he could not drive the car backwards much longer.

The road was winding just before they would get to the town. No one was shooting at them but that still did not mean they weren't following them.

When Jon got to the town he found the doctor right away. There was as sign outside in the yard. Jon carried Ruth up the steps and did not knock at the door. He went inside and called for the doctor. An elderly man came rushing from a room to the left. He took one look at Jon and Ruth said, "Follow me."

Jon put Ruth on the table and sat in a chair next to it holding her hand. The doctor did not tell him to leave. He examined the wound and called for someone. An elderly woman appeared at the door. "I need your help."

The woman nodded and pulled bandages from a drawer and brought instruments for the doctor to use.

Ruth had a bullet in her shoulder. The doctor removed the bullet, stitched the wound, and bandaged it. Then he turned to Jon and told him to take off his shirt. Jon did as he was told. The doctor tended to his arm. Jon never took his eyes off of Ruth.

The doctor said, "She'll be all right. You want to tell me what happened?

Jon shook his head. "I don't know. We had a quarrel. I left her to come back to town and I heard a gunshot. I ran back and found her on the ground with a bullet in her."

"You know I have to report this."

Jon nodded.

Ruth opened her eyes and saw Jon. "Jon."

"You are going to be all right Ruth. The doctor said so."

Ruth smiled and tried to sit up. Jon pushed her back down. "Easy sweetheart. The doc just took a bullet out of you."

"We have to get out of here."

"Ruth do you know who shot you?"

Ruth nodded. "We need to get back to my cabin."

Jon turned to the doctor. "I know you have to report this, but could you give us 24 hours? I'm General Raymond, US. Army Intelligence and this is Ms. Ruth Cummings. We need some time doc."

The doctor looked at Ruth. "I've read all your books. I can't give you more than 24 hours."

"Good enough."

Jon helped Ruth up and carried her to the car. The doctor gave him some medicine for fever, and he drove as fast as he could to the cabin. He stopped a quarter mile from the cabin. "Ruth. I am not sure how safe the cabin is. I am going to carry you the rest of the way. They may be waiting for the car."

Ruth nodded and opened the passenger door to get out. A shot hit the car on the passenger side. Ruth quickly closed the door and leaned over in the seat.

Jon swore and started the car and drove as fast as he could to the cabin. He stopped the car as close to the cabin as he could get with the passenger door facing the Cabin. Jon got out, keeping low he moved around to the passenger door. He opened it and Ruth climbed out with Jon following her. They got up the steps and were going through the door when a bullet hit the doorframe.

Jon pushed Ruth inside and she fell on the floor. Jon closed and locked the door. He picked Ruth up and took her to the couch. He went through every room making sure the windows were locked and the kitchen door was the only extra exit from the house.

After he was sure that all was locked he went back to Ruth. "Ruth. Do you have any weapons here?"

Ruth nodded and pointed to the study and said, "Behind the bookcase is a secret room. Help me up and I'll show you."

Jon helped her up and carried her to the study. He put her in a chair, and she directed him how to move the bookcase and get to the secret room.

Jon found an arsenal. He took weapons out and bullets. He put a knife in his belt. He took the weapons back to the living room and went back for Ruth.

The living room was too open. They needed a place that was more secure. He looked at the loft and went up the stairs. The loft had two bedrooms. There were too many blind spots up there. He checked the windows again and went back to Ruth.

"Ruth are there anymore secret rooms or anything in this place?"

Ruth shook her head.

Jon did not like it, but this was the best room that gave him full view of all sides of the house. The downstairs bedroom was a blind spot, but he could lock the door and have time to protect them before anyone broke down the door.

Jon checked on Ruth and found that she was developing a fever. He had to get her away from the cabin and into a hospital.

He gave her some medicine the doctor gave him and asked her. "Ruth who shot you?"

"Reinhardt."

"We need to get out of here. Is there anyone you trust we can call for help?"

"Brady and Rosco."

"How do we reach them?"

"In the study. Computer. Send email. Help me up. It's a secret code."

Jon helped Ruth to the study. She sat at the computer and entered a series of codes. She waited until she got a response.

Ruth answered and then shut off the computer. "They will be here in three hours."

Ruth slumped in the chair. Jon carried her to the couch and gave her some water. He went to the window. Nothing moved. He went to each window and looked out. Nothing. He was beginning to think he had imagined the bullets hitting the car until he heard something upstairs.

He checked on Ruth. She was sleeping. He moved up the stairs careful not to make a sound. He heard movement and pressed himself to the wall next to the bedroom door. The knob turned. Jon wanted him alive.

When the door opened. Jon tackled the man to the ground. He knocked him unconscious and dragged him downstairs to tie him up.

Ruth was awake and watched him drag the unconscious man down the stairs. Jon tied him up and put him in the corner.

Ruth lay back down on the couch.

It was the longest three hours of Jon's life.

Someone called from the woods surrounding the house. Ruth was awake and said it was Brady. Jon told them to show themselves. Brady and Rosco came out of the woods with their hands up.

Jon told them to come in. Brady and Rosco put their hands down and called for the ambulance.

Jon rode with the ambulance to the hospital holding Ruth's hand all the way. When they reached the hospital, they took Ruth into a room and made Jon wait in the waiting room.

The doctor soon came out and said she would be fine. They were keeping her for a few days. Jon shook the doctor's hand and left the waiting room heading for the exit. The doctor stopped him by asking, "Don't you want to see her? She was asking for you?"

Jon shook his head and went to his office. He thought he knew who the person was that was leaking information. When he got to his office Lt. Russell was looking though his papers.

Jon pulled his weapon and said, "Looking for something?"

Lt. Russell put his hands-on top of his head.

Ruth got out of the hospital and went in search for Jon. She went to his apartment and knocked on the door.

When he opened the door, he was surprised. He did not expect to see her again. He did not ask her in but said, "What do you want? Your son has been released."

"I'd like to talk to you."

"I think you said it all Ruth."

"No. You did not let me finish what I was saying before you left."

"Ruth…"

"I love you."

Jon stared at her. What did she want now? "You don't have to say that Ruth. If there is something you want me to do for you just ask. Don't lie to me. I know you were only doing what you did because of your son."

Ruth stared at him for a moment then smiled. "Actually, there is something I want you to do."

Jon nodded and let her into his apartment.

He asked if she wanted to sit down, but she asked him to put on some music. Jon nodded and put on the same CD that they danced to.

When he realized it was the same CD he said, "I am sorry. I will change it."

Ruth said, "No. What I want is for you to dance with me."

Jon stared at her and shook his head. "No. Ruth what do you want?"

Ruth walked to him put her arms around his neck and said, "Kiss me."

Jon tried to push her away then stopped. He put his arms around her and kissed her back.

Jon ended the kiss and said, "Damn you Ruth." He tried to push her away again, but she held on.

"Jon. Listen to me. We knew the leak was from your office. It could have been anyone. I knew the night you came to my apartment that it wasn't you. I love you. Everything we did together was because I love you."

Jon looked into her eyes. Searching for the truth.

Ruth kissed him again and he found it.

Love Me For Who I Am

"Love me without fear. Trust me without questioning. Need me without demanding. Want me without restrictions. Accept me without change. Love me for who I am."
Anonymous -

To Everyone that believes in Love and for those that need more convincing.

Clarissa was excited. She was going to America. Her sister's fiancée had sent her a letter asking her to come to America and Clarissa was to accompany her.

When she first heard that she was going she did not understand why her sister would want her near her, but when she was told that she would be her sister's maid for the trip, Clarissa understood why she was being allowed to go.

No one would know who she was or that she was Elizabeth's sister. She remembered when she first heard she would be going. She received a summons to see her father in his study a month ago.

Clarissa dressed very carefully. She was not allowed to be seen or announced as a member of the family since she was ten. She had fallen down the stairs and her leg did not heal right. She limped and that was a disgrace to the family. She was treated like a servant and made to work in the stables at times. She loved the horses and rode often. She had made friends with the other servants and had learned a lot from them. She could cook, sew, ride, shoot a gun, work in the garden and her grandmother taught her how to read and write.

She worked hard but she liked it better than what her sisters did. They had servants wait on them and dressed for balls and dinners. They did not read or write, could not cook and when they rode, they rode sidesaddle and only for an hour or so. Clarissa was used to riding all day.

She had learned from old Mason about how to take care of horses when they were sick, and even taught her how to train a horse to do tricks.

She was nervous about seeing her father. She had not spoken to him or her mother for over a year. And that was only for a few minutes, when one of her sisters said she saw her peeking through some drapes to see the people at the party they had, when her parents announced the engagement of her sister Melissa to Lord Weatherton.

She tried to think of what she had done wrong but could not think of anything. When she arrived in the study, she was surprised to see her sister Elizabeth was there also. Elizabeth was the one who disliked her most.

Clarissa's father did not rise when she entered the room but motioned for her to come closer to his desk.

Elizabeth looked at her in disgust as she limped across the room to her father.

Clarissa said, "Yes father? You wanted to see me?"

Clarissa's father said, "Yes. You will be accompanying Elizabeth to America. You will be leaving in a month's time and will be going to California."

Clarissa's eyes widened in surprise. She knew better than to say anything. So, she nodded.

Elizabeth said, "You will accompany me as my maid. You are not to tell anyone that we are related in any way. You will return here when we reach California. I will not have you living in my house."

Clarissa nodded and asked her father, "May I take my horse?"

Her father hesitated before answering. This was his chance to get rid of her. He could afford to be generous. "Yes, but do not take much more. Elizabeth will need space for her trunks. Now leave."

Clarissa left the study and ran as fast as she could to see Mason. He had been to America and could tell her about the trip to California.

Mason told her about the Indians, the desert, and camping. He said they would land in New York and take a wagon train to California.

Clarissa went to see her grandmother and read every book she could find about America.

When it was time to leave Clarissa had only taken one bag while Elizabeth had packed ten trunks.

Elizabeth was very demanding and let Clarissa know her duties.

On the trip to New York, Elizabeth stayed in the stateroom, while Clarissa stayed in the servant's quarters. She did not mind because she could see Aristotle each day. He did not like the boat at first, but she spent a lot of time with him and he settled down.

When they reached New York, Elizabeth stayed at the hotel for a few days, to rest from the trip, before starting the journey to California.

Clarissa was excited about the city and made many new friends. She walked on the docks and visited the shops. She wished she had some money, but Elizabeth said she did not need any.

She rode Aristotle out of the city and across the countryside every day. It was beautiful.

Her father had made arrangements for them to purchase a wagon, team, and driver to take them to California. Elizabeth did not like the driver and fired him. She said that they did not need him because Clarissa could drive the team.

They left with a group that was traveling to Missouri to meet up with a wagon train heading West.

By the time they had arrived Clarissa was very good in handling the oxen and had even named them. She tied Aristotle to the back of the wagon. She rode him for a while each night after she was through taking care of Elizabeth.

Elizabeth complained every day about everything, but Clarissa did not mind. She was so engrossed in the adventure.

When they arrived in Missouri, Elizabeth stayed in a hotel room while Clarissa stayed with the wagon. Clarissa went down to sign them up for the trip and saw the most beautiful man she had ever seen.

He was leaning against the wall to the left of the table where you were to join the wagon train. He looked at her and nodded. She smiled at him and looked away quickly. She knew anyone like him would not be interested in a woman with a limp. No man would.

Trevor saw the young woman and could not take his eyes off of her. She was the most beautiful woman he had ever seen. He wondered whom she was traveling with. It would be a long way to California. He watched her hands, as she signed the contract to join the train. He did not see any ring on her finger. He would look later to find out her name. He thought it strange that a woman would sign the contract and not her husband or the man in charge of their wagons.

His father, Jason Cummings, was sitting at the desk and was questioning her when she handed him the contract. "Lady Elizabeth Warthing and Clarissa." His father looked at her and asked, "Is there no man to accompany you?"

Clarissa shook her head.

His father looked at her and asked, "Who is driving your team?"

Clarissa said, "I am. I drove the team from New York. I handled, James, Beth, Jason, Aaron, Ruby, and Violet very well. They are really very tame."

Jason lowered his head and smiled. She named the oxen. And by her accent she was from Europe. She did not know how hard the trip would be. "I am sorry Miss, but if you do not have a man to accompany you I am afraid you cannot take the wagon train. Every man will be busy taking care of his own wagon and not have time for anyone else."

Clarissa shook her head and said, "I do not require assistance and would not burden anyone. If I fall behind you can leave us. I will get Elizabeth to California alone if I have to, but I am going to California."

Jason stared at this woman for a minute than looked at his son. He raised an eyebrow when he saw that his son was watching the woman with some interest. Well. Finally. Trent would be thirty soon and this was the first time he has shown any interest in a woman in some time. He would put her in the middle of the wagon train and watch out for her himself, if she could get his son interested in a woman to give him some grandchildren.

"All right Miss Clarissa. I will put you in the middle of the train. But if you cannot keep up or have trouble we will drop you off at the nearest town."

Clarissa smiled and said, "Thank you sir. What is your name?"

"Jason Cummings."

"Thank you Mr. Cummings. I will not be any trouble."

After Clarissa left Trent followed her out of the building. He did not know why but he wanted to see where she would go. He thought she would go to the hotel, but she turned and went to where to wagons were. She stopped at one of the wagons and went inside. When she came out she was wearing a pair of men's pants and boots. She went to the other side of the wagon and came back around leading the most beautiful horse he had ever seen. She mounted and rode away with a grace of someone who was born in the saddle.

Trent went to the stables and saddled his horse. He wanted to see where she was going.

Clarissa was thinking of the man that she saw earlier when she noticed a rider coming towards her. She reached for her rifle and laid it across her lap.

Trent pulled up on his horse and approached her slowly. He noticed she had pulled her rifle and had laid it across her lap.

Interesting. This woman intrigued him more and more. Did she know how to use it?

He stopped a few feet away, tipped his hat, and said, "Afternoon ma'am. Nice day for a ride."

Clarissa did not say anything but nodded.

Trent did not know what to say. Then he remembered how she had named the oxen and asked, "You are Clarissa aren't you? I am Trent. I overheard that you named the oxen driving your team. I was wondering what you named your horse."

Clarissa looked at him and smiled. "Aristotle. What did you name yours?"

Trevor laughed. Aristotle. "Nothing that fancy. I call him Red."

Clarissa put away her rifle and got down from her horse. She walked over to Red and put her hand on his nose so he could smell her.

Trevor got off his horse and watched her.

Clarissa ran her hand over the horse feeling his muscles as she went. When she got to his front right leg, she paused and got down on her knees. She looked at his foot and picked it up. "He has a bruise here. You need to soak it for a day or so and do not ride him hard for at least a week."

She rose and checked his flank and legs. When she was satisfied that the horse was well she returned to her own and mounted.

Trent watched her. How could she tell that Red had a stone bruise two days ago by looking at his legs like that? "How did you know that?"

Clarissa shrugged and said, "I worked with horses quite often, and Mason taught me all he knew. You can tell by the muscle form on his leg. It was tight because he was hurting when he put pressure where the bruise was. You take good care of him. He is fine everywhere else."

Trent nodded and said, "Thanks." He did not want to let her get away and he could see that she was already moving her horse towards town. "Would you come by the stables and check on him later? I do not want anything to happen to him before the wagon train leaves."

Clarissa stopped Aristotle and said, "You are going on the wagon train to California?"

He did not want her to know who he was just yet. Too many times women were interested in his money instead of him. "Yes, I am going to scout for them."

Clarissa smiled and said, "That sounds interesting. I have to go now but I would like to ask you what it is like. When would you like for me to take a look at Red?"

"This evening after dinner. I am staying at the Clarion House Hotel. Their stables are behind it."

Clarissa nodded. That was where Elizabeth was staying. "I can meet you there. What time?"

"How about 8 o'clock?"

Clarissa nodded again and rode Aristotle back to the wagon. If he had enough money to stay at the Clarion House then he probably knew Elizabeth. She made it a point to know all the handsome men around her. It did not seem to bother her that she was engaged and on the way to meet her fiancée. She would see to his horse and maybe they would be friends but when he saw that she was only Elizabeth's maid he would not want to be seen with her.

Clarissa helped Elizabeth prepare for a dinner engagement and was leaving the hotel when she ran into Trent. She tried to move away so that he would not see her, but he called her name. "Clarissa."

Elizabeth was about to enter the dining room and turned to see who had called Clarissa.

Clarissa knew Elizabeth would be angry, but she could not be rude to Trent. "Hello Trent."

Trent saw that she was nervous and did not know why. And why was she at the hotel? Was she looking for him? "What are you doing here?"

Before Clarissa could answer, Elizabeth moved to stand between them and said, "She is my maid. How do you know her?"

Trent did not like the woman who moved between him and Clarissa. He did not want to answer her, but he could not be rude. "We met this afternoon."

Elizabeth turned to Clarissa and said harshly, "We will talk tomorrow. Go back to the wagon and stay there."

Clarissa lowered her head and left the hotel quickly. She had never been so embarrassed. Trent would never speak to her now or meet her later. She would see to his horse for him. She hoped that Elizabeth would not be too angry tomorrow.

Trent let her leave, but he would speak with her later. He hoped she would still meet him to see to his horse. He did not speak to the woman that was mean to Clarissa and joined his father in the dining room. He was surprised to see the woman that he had just met came to their table. His father held her chair for her to join them.

Elizabeth was surprised to see the man that was talking to Clarissa at their table.

Jason could feel the tension at the table and made introductions. "Trent may I introduce Lady Elizabeth Warthing from England. She and her maid are traveling to California with us on the wagon train."

Trevor nodded but said nothing. She was beautiful to look at, but he did not like the way she treated Clarissa.

Trent did not stay to have dinner. He excused himself and left the dining room.

Jason was surprised at his son's behavior. Something must have happened between them for him to be rude to her.

Trent went to the stables before 8 o'clock to see to Red. He did not think that Clarissa would show up. But when he arrived he found her with Red and she was wrapping a cloth around his horse's leg. She did not see him, and he watched her for a while before approaching. "Hello. I did not think you were going to come."

Clarissa was startled out of her thoughts when she heard his voice. She looked up at him and only stared. She turned back to his horse and dipped the cloth in the solution she had made and re-wrapped his leg before she spoke. "I did not think you would come."

Trevor came closer and asked, "Why? I said I would."

Clarissa shrugged her shoulders and did not answer.

Trent watched her for a moment before asking, "Have you eaten dinner yet?"

Clarissa shook her head. She did not feel like eating. She did not mind Elizabeth and the rest of the family treating her like they did, but she did not want Trent to think badly of her.

"Can I buy you dinner then?"

Clarissa looked at him in surprise. "I thought you had dinner already?"

"No. I did not like the company. Your Lady Elizabeth was sitting at our table. I did not like the way she talked to you."

Clarissa shook her head and said, "I am her maid for the trip Trent. When we get to California, I will be going back home. It is not so bad. She will stay here. I can go back to what I always do."

Trent wanted to know more but she did not answer him about buying her dinner. "I know a place we can eat that is away from Lady Elizabeth. Will you join me?"

Clarissa was going to say no but changed her mind. Once she was back in England she would never see him again and she knew this was her only chance to live before she was hidden away again. "Yes, Trent. I would like that."

Trent offered her his hand, and she took it. He pulled her to her feet and held her hand longer than necessary before he released it.

Trent took her to a restaurant that was quiet and away from the hotel. It bordered on the wrong side of town but as long as she was with him, she would be all right.

Clarissa liked the little restaurant. They ordered their dinner and she asked him about being a scout. Trevor told her some stories about when he was learning to be a scout and what he looked for. She listened with interest. When their meals came, they ate, and he asked her about what she did in England.

"Oh, I did a lot of different things. I helped Mason take care of the horses when they become ill or have problems. I cooked when the cook had her day off; I sewed on occasion when there was a need. I tended the gardens with Jacob. He is getting old and the young ones that help him are careless. I rode Aristotle every day and I did whatever else was needed."

"So, you are not usually a maid?" Trent asked.

"No. Elizabeth wanted me to come on the trip with her and be her maid. She is going to California to meet her fiancée. When we get there, I will be sent back to Warthing House."

Trent did not like that. He wanted her to stay in California. "Why did you name your horse Aristotle? Isn't that a strange name for a horse?"

Clarissa laughed and said, "I liked reading what Aristotle said. My grandmother has a large library and she taught me to read and write. I have read almost every book she has."

Trent listened to Clarissa and knew there was more than what she was saying. There was something about her that said she was not just a servant and if her grandmother had a library that large then she had to have money. So, if she had money why was Clarissa only a servant for Lady Elizabeth?

He looked at Clarissa as she was talking and then he realized what it was that caused him to question her only being a servant.

If she were dressed like Elizabeth, they could pass as sisters. He shook his head. That was crazy. If she were Elizabeth's sister, she would not be her maid.

Clarissa realized it was getting late and she had a lot of shopping to do tomorrow for supplies for the trip to California.

"Trent, thank you for a wonderful dinner but it is getting late and I have to go shopping tomorrow for supplies for the trip to California."

"Do you know what to get? It will be a long trip. Maybe I should come with you to make sure you get the right things."

Clarissa smiled. She knew she should not, but Elizabeth would never be seen in the shops that she was going to visit. "I would like that. Thank you."

Trent smiled and asked, "What time are you going to go shopping?"

"I have to get some money from Elizabeth first. She does not wake until noon. So, I suppose it would have to be in the afternoon."

"Will you go riding with me in the morning?"

Clarissa shook her head. "You cannot take Red. He needs at least another day for his leg to heal properly. I will put some more wraps on it in the morning."

"I have another horse I can use. His name is Buster."

Clarissa laughed. "Buster?"

Trent shrugged.

"All right. I would like to ride in the morning. Meet me at my wagon at 9 am."

Trent smiled and said, "All right and after our ride I will take you to lunch."

Clarissa smiled and nodded.

The next morning Trent arrived at Clarissa's wagon and she was gone. Her horse was there but she was nowhere around. He waited a little while and then asked someone in the next wagon if they had seen her.

"Yes, she was up early like she always is. Then two men came and took her away. I tried to stop them, but they told me to mind my own business."

Trent did not like what he heard. "How long ago did they take her? Did they say anything about where they were taking her?"

The old woman said, "They took her about an hour ago. They said that Lady Elizabeth was not happy with her and she would pay."

Trent ran to this horse and rode back to town. When he arrived at the hotel he asked which room belonged to Elizabeth Warthing.

Trevor raced up the stairs to her room and knocked on the door. Elizabeth soon answered.

Trent did not enter the room but said in an angry tone, "Where is Clarissa?"

"I do not care for your tone and it is none of your business where she is. She is being punished for disobeying me."

Trent had never hit a woman in his life, but if she did not tell him where Clarissa was, he would be tempted now. "Where is she? Tell me know." Trent had never been so angry.

Elizabeth stepped back and said, "She is in the stables where she belongs."

Trent ran to the stables and found her in a vacant stall. She was so still he was afraid he was too late. He knelt beside her and ran his hands over her arms and down her legs. He did not feel anything broken but they had beaten her pretty badly. He picked her up gently and he carried to the doctor's office.

Trent waited while the doctor examined her. Half an hour later, the doctor came out of the examining room. "Well, she has a broken rib, some cuts, and bruises, but she will be all right. She put up a good fight and thank God they did not do anything but beat her. She will heal in time, but she will need rest for a few days. Is she going on the wagon train?"

Trent nodded.

The doctor shook his head. "You are supposed to leave tomorrow aren't you?"

Trent nodded again.

The doctor sighed, "Well if she does she can't do anything for a while. That broken rib needs to heal. She has to stay in bed for at least three or four days, and with the way those wagons are if she cannot stay here, then she will have to rest for at least a week."

Trent said, "I will make sure she rests for at least a week."

The doctor nodded and let him see her.

Clarissa was in pain. It hurt to breath and she hurt all over. She tried to smile when she saw Trent, but it hurt too much. "Sorry…Trent. I missed…our…ride."

Trent held her hand and said, "Don't worry there will be other rides. The doctor said that you have to rest three or four days, and if you leave on the wagon train tomorrow, you have to rest for a week before you can do anything."

Clarissa shook her head. "Can't. Have to…shop…for supplies. Drive…wagon."

Trent shook his head, "No you can't. If you must go on the wagon train I will get the supplies and drive the wagon."

Clarissa shook her head again. "No. You…scout."

Trent sighed. She was right. He could not drive her wagon and scout for the train. He would get one of his men to drive the team. "I have someone that will drive the team. But I want your promise that you will not do anything for at least a week."

Clarissa shook her head again. "Eliza…beth."

"You let me take care of Elizabeth."

Clarissa did not answer but closed her eyes and went to sleep.

Trent carried Clarissa to the hotel and put her in his bed. While she slept he purchased supplies for the trip and told his father about what Elizabeth had done. His father was angry and told him that one of his men would drive their wagon and not to worry about Elizabeth he would take care of her.

Trent moved Clarissa to the wagon the next morning and put her inside. His father must have talked to Elizabeth, because she did not say anything when he put Clarissa on the bed in the wagon. He still did not trust her.

Raymond drove the wagon for Clarissa and Elizabeth. By the third day, he refused to drive the wagon if Elizabeth sat next to him on the seat. She complained constantly.

Trent came by each day to check on Clarissa and see that she was being treated well. They moved her wagon to the number two position behind his fathers' wagon. He still did not trust Elizabeth. The evening of the third day Clarissa told Trent that she was well enough to sit on the seat next to Raymond. Trent knew why she was doing this but asked Ray to watch her. If she looked tired, he was supposed to help her into the back so she could rest.

Raymond liked Clarissa and was eager to have her sitting next to him. They talked about a lot of things.

Trent did not like it that Ray was so close to Clarissa. They were getting along well, too well. He had never been jealous in his life and he did not like the feeling. Clarissa was his. She evidently did not know that.

By the end of the first week on the trail, Clarissa was feeling better and could not understand Trent's mood. Had she done something wrong? She would ask him that night when he came by to see her. When he did not come to see her, she went in search for him.

"Mr. Cummings have you seen Trent?" Clarissa asked.

"He walked over to the stream a little while ago."

Clarissa thanked him and walked to the stream. She found Trent sitting on the grass overlooking the water.

"Trent have I done something to make you angry with me?"

Trent turned his head to look at her. "No. How are you feeling?"

Clarissa joined him on the grass and looked out over the water. "I am feeling better. I asked Raymond to let me drive tomorrow to see how it would feel. He is nice. I like him."

Trent did not say anything for a long while then sighed and said, "I am sorry for acting like I have been the past few days." He paused before continuing. "I have never been jealous before and I do not like it."

Clarissa looked at him in surprise. "Jealous? Of what?"

Trent said, "Of you and Raymond."

Clarissa shook her head and said, "I do not understand. Raymond is just a friend. He is easy to talk to. He treats me like a person. He does not mind that I have a limp."

Trent looked at Clarissa and frowned. "What about your limp? There are a lot of wonderful things about you. I hardly noticed it."

Clarissa nodded and said, "Where I come from it means a lot. When I was ten I fell down the stairs and broke my leg. It did not heal right, and my family sees me as embarrassment."

Trent stared at her for a moment before he asked, "How old are you?"

Clarissa said, "Twenty."

"My father went to England once and told me that the young women have what is known as a season. They are paraded before the Lords and Earls hoping to be selected for a wife. Did you ever have a season?"

Clarissa laughed and said, "You must be joking. My family hides me away. The thought of me parading before Lords and Earls would devastate them. They would be laughed out of society. They have three other daughters to think about. They all married well." Then she paused before continuing. "Well except one. She is meeting her fiancée."

Trevor thought back to the time they had dinner and said, "So your other sister is meeting her fiancée in California?"

Clarissa did not think before she answered. "Yes." Then she realized what she said and pleaded. "Trent you must not tell anyone. Elizabeth would be devastated if anyone knew I was her sister."

Trent shook his head and said, "So you are Lady Clarissa Warthing. Why do you let them treat you like that?"

Clarissa sighed and said, "Trent you do not understand. I have nowhere to go and it is not so bad. They leave me alone to do what I want as long as I stay away from them."

"What about getting married some day? Don't you want that?"

Clarissa looked out over the water and said, "It is not good to wish for what you cannot have Trent. I am a cripple. No man with any substance would have me. I would be an embarrassment." Then she smiled and looked at him and said, "Besides, I have a full life on the country estate. I care for the horses, ride each day, and talk to whomever I want. I can wear what I want and read as many books as I care to read."

Trent looked at her and said, "You are an amazing woman. Any man would be proud to have you as his wife."

Clarissa shook her head and said, "Not in my country and when Elizabeth meets her fiancée in California I will have to go back. I have no money." She thought for a moment then said, "You know Trent. I really do not want to go back. I like your America. Do you think I could get a job somewhere in California and stay here?"

Trent did not answer right away. He wanted her to stay but did not know why and his feelings were confusing to him. He did not know if he loved her or why he felt protective of her. "I suppose you could."

Trent and Clarissa sat by the stream looking at the water for a long while in silence before Clarissa stood and said, "Good night Trent." And went back to the Wagon.

She let Elizabeth have the bed in the wagon and slept on the ground. The next morning, she felt stiff, but her ribs felt better. She drove only half the day before her ribs started hurting.

Each night she would walk away from the wagons with Trent and they would talk. She really enjoyed the time with him.

Raymond stayed and drove the wagon for them for the first month of the trip. She was feeling better and could do everything that needed to be done. Raymond asked if she would take a walk with him after dinner and Clarissa accepted. She would be back in time to see Trent.

Trent came to the wagon to see Clarissa and found her gone. Elizabeth was pleased to tell him that he was too late that Clarissa had gone off with Raymond.

Trent was angry and went looking for them. He found them and did not like what he saw. Raymond and Clarissa were standing in a clearing and he watched Raymond kiss her. He left and went back to the wagons.

Clarissa moved away from Raymond and said, "Raymond I think of you as a friend. Can we be friends?"

Raymond had come to care for Clarissa, but he could see that she did not share the feelings he had so he nodded.

Raymond did not drive the wagon after that night. Clarissa was feeling better and drove the wagon during the day. She had not seen Trent in several days. She was tired after the long day of driving the oxen and fell asleep each night missing Trent.

They were on the trail for three months and they had stopped for a rest during the day when she heard a woman's scream. She ran as fast as she could and saw that a child had fallen down the side of a mountain. She quickly ran back to the wagon, took a rope, tied it to a tree, and was sliding down the hill to reach the child by the time the men had arrived.

Trent watched her as she slid down the to the child. Everyone stayed away from the edge as far as they could.

Clarissa reached the child and saw that his leg was broken. He looked to be about 4 years old. She tried to calm the crying child and looked for other injuries.

"You are going to be all right. I have to get you back up the mountain. Can you put your arms around my neck?"

The child nodded through his tears and Clarissa picked up the child.

Trent called to her. "Clarissa I am coming down to help you." When he started down there were several rocks that were loose and showered down the mountain.

Clarissa said, "No. The rocks are too loose here. I can bring him up."

Clarissa carried the child piggyback and made her way up the mountain. The men pulled on the rope to help her. When she arrived at the top, she put the child down and looked at his leg. "Do we have a doctor on the train?"

Trent said, "No."

Clarissa looked at the child's leg and sighed. It was a bad break. "Let's get him to his wagon. I can set the leg, but we will have to watch him for a few days. Also have someone get my black bag from my wagon."

Trent nodded and picked up the child and had someone fetch her bag.

Clarissa gave the child something for pain and set the leg. She sewed up the break in the skin and gave instructions to the mother on what to do for the next few days. She left some ointment, to put on the leg, to ward off infection and checked on him twice a day for the next few days. She was relieved to see that it was healing. The mother thanked her.

Clarissa had not seen Trent except for the accident and missed him. She walked out to a nearby stream later that night. They were told to stay near the wagons because they were in Indian Territory, but she did not think. She had to get away from Elizabeth and think about Trent.

She was deep in thought when someone grabbed her from behind and threw her onto a horse in front of someone. She did not scream, there was no time. She was held tight in front of a man and there were several horses riding with them. They rode until dawn and Clarissa could see that they were in an Indian camp.

She was taken from the horse and put in a teepee. She did not know what to do so she stayed there in silence. She had heard stories and she was afraid. It was noon before anyone came to her.

She was taken from her teepee to another one where there were several women. There was a child lying on a blanket on the ground. She did not know what she was supposed to do but when she saw the child, she went over to him and knelt beside him.

She checked his head for fever and found that he was burning up. She quickly removed the blanket covering him and checked him over and found that his leg was broken and infected. She did not think that no one stopped her as she began to work on the leg. She would have to clean out the infection before she set it. She always wore a pouch with her medicines in it and she was thankful of that now. She never knew when she would need some of her healing herbs. She asked for water.

She did not know their language, but they managed to communicate. She cleaned the wound and set the leg. She tore some of her petticoat and asked for two sticks. They brought her what she needed, she made a drink for the boy, and he drank. When she was finished, she sat back and looked at the Indians around her. She did not know what would happen next.

A blanket was moved close to the boy and they brought her some food. She sat on the blanket and ate the food. After three days, the boy's fever broke, and she could see that his leg was healing.

She had not been out of the teepee except to relieve herself in three days. She was allowed to walk around the camp and wandered to the horses. She looked them over and found one that was hurt. She walked over to him and put her hand on his nose so that he could smell her. She talked softly to him and ran her hands over him gently. The Indians gathered around her and watched.

She tended to his wound and then moved to another horse and then another. Checking them all to make sure they were all right. When she was satisfied, she went back to the teepee and checked on the little boy. He was awake and smiled at her.

She did not now how long she had been in their camp, but she guessed that it had been a week now. She did not know what would happen to her, but at least they treated her kindly.

Trent was worried. When they found Clarissa was gone, he searched the area and found the horses tracks around the stream. He could not leave the train to look for her. It had been a week now. He realized that he loved her and that he should have not stayed away from her as he did. He was angry that she let Raymond kiss her, but he had never said anything to her about how he felt about her or kissed her. He wanted to but did not know if she would have wanted him too. Now he would never have the chance.

Clarissa woke the next morning and was taken from the teepee to the horses. She did not understand at first but one of the braves put her on a horse and several others also mounted. They rode out of the camp. She did not know where they were taking her, but they rode for several days before she could see the wagon train. One of the Indians said something to her, and they left her there.

Trent saw her with the Indians and could not move. He did not know what to think. She looked unharmed. When he saw that the Indians had left her and rode off, he rode quickly to her.

Clarissa saw Trent riding towards her and smiled.

When Trent reached her, he dismounted and pulled her off the horse and kissed her. Clarissa was caught by surprise but soon responded and kissed him back.

Trent ended the kiss and hugged her to him. "Clarissa. I thought I had lost you." Trent kissed her again before he released her and asked, "What happen? I saw the tracks of where they had taken you. I thought I would never see you again."

Clarissa told him about the boy and how the Indians had been kind to her.

Trent hugged her again, put her back on the horse, and rode towards the wagons.

Clarissa received a warm welcome and everything settled back into its normal pattern. Trent would come by in the evening and she would walk with him. He did not kiss her again.

After a week Clarissa asked, "Trent that day I returned to the wagons you kissed me but have not kissed me since then. Why not?"

Trent stopped and looked down at her and lied. "I do not know. I was glad to see that you were unharmed."

Clarissa lowered her head and was silent. He did not care for her the way she cared for him. He only kissed her because he had been concerned about her and was glad that she was all right.

Clarissa turned and walked back to the wagons. She would not walk with him again. It was too painful to walk with him, be with him, and not want him.

Trent did not stop her when she left. He did not know why he lied to her. He wanted her like no other woman he had ever known. He shook his head and followed her. He did not understand anything anymore. If she had been any other woman, he would have already made love to her.

The next few days were long and tiring. When Trent went to see Clarissa, she said she was too tired and turned away.

Trent did not like that she would not see him but accepted it. He still did not know what was wrong with him. He wanted her yet he could not tell her.

They were only a month from California when they were close enough to a town for some of the people on the train to buy supplies. Elizabeth rode into town and sent a telegram. She had had enough of Clarissa. She would be doing the family a favor by getting rid of her. She wired her fiancée to tell him of her arrival in a month. She would hire someone to take care of Clarissa when she arrived.

Clarissa went into town to buy some supplies and saw Trent. She saw a sign in the Mercantile that said there was a shooting contest that afternoon. The prize money caught her eye. She could stay in America if she won the contest. It would give her enough to live on until she found a job.

She asked the storeowner about signing up. He laughed at her and said that she needed twenty-five cents to enter. Clarissa did not have any money but asked if there was some work that needed to be done so she could earn the money. The storeowner looked at her and rubbed his hand over his beard. He shrugged and said, "Sure."

Clarissa was taken to the back room and he set her to work. She worked for over an hour stocking the shelves and arranging the goods. When she was done, he signed her up for the contest.

Trent saw Clarissa go into the Mercantile. He wanted to talk to her and waited for her to come out. He waited for a long while then became concerned. He walked to the Mercantile and asked the owner about her. He told Trent that she was working in order to earn the money to enter the shooting contest.

Trent looked at the poster and entered the contest also. Did she really think she had a chance?

At 3 o'clock everyone that had entered the contest gathered. Everyone in town was watching as Clarissa moved with the men to the shooting line. Everyone laughed at her. She had ridden Aristotle and had her rifle. She put her rifle on the table and noticed that Trent had also entered the contest. She also noticed that he was the only one that was not laughing at her.

The contest would continue until someone missed. After each round, the target was moved further away. After 30 minutes there were only two contestants left, Trent and herself. No one was laughing at her now. Trent knew he should let her win, but something told him she would not want that.

He aimed his rifle, took a shot, and missed.

Clarissa wondered if he did it deliberately but thought of the prize money and a new chance and raised her rifle and hit the target.

Everyone cheered and the storeowner presented her with the prize money. Trent did not say anything to her and walked away.

Clarissa knew men did not like women who were intelligent and now she had beaten him in the shooting contest. She pushed the thought from her mind and held her prize money close to her chest. Now she would not have to go back with Elizabeth.

Elizabeth was in the crowd and snickered at Clarissa. She would only have to have her around for another month and then she would take her revenge for the way she had been treated on the trip. She was the daughter of an Earl and Clarissa the family embarrassment, had been treated better.

They were on the trail for another week when a group of Indians approached the wagon train. Mr. Cummings had commented that it was strange that they had not had any Indian attacks during the trip. There were Indian signs, but they did not bother them. They traveled alongside of the train out of rifle range as if they were protecting them.

Mr. Cummings ordered everyone to hold their fire. The Indians did not seem to be hostile. Since Trent knew the language, he talked to them. When he returned he spoke to Clarissa for the first time since the contest. "They want you to go with them. They call you 'healing woman.' The boy you saved was the son of a very powerful chief. They want your healing powers for one of their tribe that is ill."

Clarissa looked at the Indians then back to Trent.

Trent said, "You do not have to go."

Clarissa shook her head. "Yes, I do. Do not wait for me. I have the prize money. When I get to California I will find a job so I can stay in America." She turned away from him then turned back and said, "I will miss you Trent. I wish you the best." She kissed him on the cheek and turned away from him for the last time. She saddled Aristotle, retrieved her medicine bag, and rode towards the Indians.

Trent watched her go and felt as if his whole world had ended. He had been a fool the entire trip. He wanted to go after her, but the Indians said no one was to go with her.

He turned away and promised himself that if he ever saw her again he would tell her he loved her and ask her to marry him.

Clarissa did not know what she would find when she arrived at the Indian camp, but it was not what she thought. Several of the children were very ill. They were all in one teepee. She looked at each one and could not find anything that would tell her what was wrong. There were no wounds or bites.

That meant that it was a sickness from within the body. She walked around the camp. It was clean. There was nothing that would tell her how the children became ill.

Then she saw a bush with red berries on it. She knelt down and examined the berries. She had read something in one of her grandmother's books about poison plants. She took the berries back to camp and was trying to ask about them when one of the squaws spoke to her in English. It seems that the children were playing near the bush and became ill shortly afterwards.

Clarissa told the squaw to let everyone know to stay away from the bush and made a drink for the children from the herbs in her bag. With the help of two other squaws, she had the fever down and the children resting peacefully after three days. She made a broth for the children to drink until they were better.

She had been in the camp for two weeks before the children were running around and playing. Clarissa smiled and played with them. She did not want to leave but she knew that she had to.

The squaw that spoke English told her that she could visit them anytime and was always welcome.

Clarissa had an escort until they saw civilization. Clarissa sat alone and looked at the town of San Francisco. She was afraid. She was accepted by the Indians and felt safe. But she knew that she could not live with them. She moved Aristotle forward and began another chapter in her life.

Trent was watching for Clarissa. They had arrived in San Francisco only the day before, but he knew she would find her way back. He also knew that she would find the wagon she used on the trip. She would save her money and live in the wagon until she found work.

Clarissa found the wagon and was asleep inside when she heard a horse approaching. She dressed quickly and reached for her rifle. When she saw that it was Trent she did not move. She did not know what he wanted.

Trent saw her and did not move. She was beautiful. How had he ever let her go without telling her how much he loved her?

Trent dismounted and approached Clarissa.

Clarissa set her rifle down and climbed out of the wagon. She had to find work and did not have time for anyone. "What do you want Trent?"

Trent stopped. Was he too late? "I came to tell you that I love you and want you to be my wife."

Clarissa looked at him in surprise and them realized what he was doing. He was trying to protect her and give her a place to live. He could not possibly love her. Clarissa shook her head and said, "No you do not. Trent I will be fine. I have some money and I will find work."

"Clarissa I am serious. I do love you. I know I have been a fool, but I do not want to spend the rest of my life without you."

Clarissa shook her head again, but Trevor closed the distance and kissed her. Clarissa put her arms around his neck and kissed him back. He had kissed her before but never like this. He was hungry for her and could not get enough.

He picked her up, put her in the back of the wagon, and climbed in after her. He undressed her and made love to her like he had dreamed of for months.

Clarissa felt like she had gone to heaven. It felt so right to love Trent and lay in his arms.

"Will you marry me Clarissa? Do you think you can learn to love me just a little?

Clarissa smiled at him and said, "I already love you Trent. I have for a long time."

Trent made love to her again. He told her to rest and that he would be back in a few hours. He would find a preacher and be back for her.

Clarissa got dressed and was brushing Aristotle when two men grabbed her. She screamed but one of the men put his hand over her mouth.

When Trent returned he could not find Clarissa. Aristotle was there but the brush that Clarissa used on him was on the ground. His first thought was of Elizabeth.

Trevor raced to the hotel to confront Elizabeth. He found her with her fiancée in the dining room. He approached them and asked her where Clarissa was. The fiancée rose in challenge until Trent introduced himself. The man sat down, and Elizabeth looked at her fiancée in shock. "What is the matter with you Herbert? This man is verbally attacking me."

Herbert put his napkin on the table and said, "My dear this man and his family owns half of San Francisco. I would suggest that if you intend to live here you had better answer him."

Elizabeth looked at Trent in bewilderment. Then realized what Herbert was saying. Their future in this town depended on this man. Elizabeth said, "They have taken her out of the city. Ten miles north of town there is a little cabin. You will find her there."

Trent left quickly and rode towards the cabin. He knew where it was. He had built it himself.

Clarissa did not know where they were taking her, but she knew Trent would come for her. They arrived at the cabin and the men took her inside. They tied her to the bed and sat at the table drinking whiskey. They were looking over at her and Clarissa did not like the way they were looking at her.

Then she heard a taping on the window. She looked at the men at the table. They did not hear it. She looked at the window and saw an Indian brave. She nodded and then she looked at the men at the table.

Soon there was a commotion outside and one of the men went to see what it was. When he did not come back, the other man became nervous. He went to the door and stepped outside. There was a gunshot and he fell face down in the doorway.

Clarissa was afraid until she saw the Indian braves come into the cabin. She remembered them from the tribe where she helped the sick children.

They untied her and removed the man from the doorway. Then they left her. She did not understand why they left until she heard a horse approaching. She opened the door and saw that it was Trent.

She ran from the cabin and into his arms.

She told him what happened, and he took her back into the cabin and made love to her again.

The next morning, they were married, and she was taken to his home. She could not believe where he lived. She stopped before entering the house and said, "Trent how could you want me? I would be an embarrassment to your family. What will they say?"

Trent kissed her and said, "They are going to love you. We do not judge people on appearances here Clarissa."

Clarissa was nervous but she would trust Trent. If she became an embarrassment to him, she would leave.

The next day Trent took her shopping, and she bought more dresses than she had ever had before. There was a dinner party that evening introducing her to his family and friends. She was nervous and afraid.

Her maid spent the afternoon preparing her. When it was time to go down to the party and dinner she looked at herself in the mirror in surprise.

Trent came to escort her down to dinner and could not move when he first saw her. She was even more beautiful that he could ever imagine.

Trent kissed her and walked with her down the stairs to the ballroom. Clarissa stopped just outside the doors and backed up. "Trent, I am afraid. I am going to embarrass you. You do not want to do this."

Trent kissed her on the cheek and said, "You are the most beautiful woman here tonight. And I cannot even imagine being with any other woman but you."

Clarissa took a deep breath and nodded.

Clarissa was having a good time and then Trent got everyone's attention and made an announcement.

"Ladies and gentlemen could I have your attention please." When everyone quieted and was looking at him Trent held out his hand for Clarissa. She walked to him and put her hand in his.

"I would like to present my wife Mrs. Clarissa Cummings formerly Lady Clarissa Warthing."

Clarissa noticed that Elizabeth and her fiancée were present, but she did not say a word. Evidently, she realized that the Cummings were important people and did not want to alienate them.

Trevor and Clarissa spent many happy years together. Neither one liked living in the city and moved to his family ranch where they raised 5 children and the best horses in the state.

Love Moves The Heart

"Love can be found in unexpected places. Sometimes we go out searching for what we think we want, and we end up with what we're supposed to have."
Kate McGahan

To Everyone that believes in Love and for those that need more convincing.

Karen could not believe this was really happening to her. Six months ago, she was working in the kitchen at an exclusive restaurant in New York and today she was in chains on a train headed for Oregon Territory.

Karen closed her eyes and thought of what had happened and the nightmare that was only beginning.

****

Six Months Earlier

Karen entered the kitchen through the service entrance as she had for the past three years. She hung up her coat in the employee's closet and put on her apron. As she entered the kitchen, she saw everyone already at work. There was a new girl working the vegetable area.

Karen did not stop to speak but went directly to her section and stared peeling potatoes. She did not have to check the schedule because she had done the same thing for three years.

She would peel potatoes, cut them up, and place them in the pot on the stove. Then she moved to the cleaning closet and took out her supplies and started cleaning the restaurant floors and waxing the tables.

She arrived each morning before sunup and did not leave until dark. Her duties involved not only the kitchen work but also cleaning the kitchen after the evening meal. It was a long day, but she needed the work.

Her mother had become ill the year before, and the doctor bills were costly.

Karen was working late one night. She was down on her hands and knees scrubbing the floor when she heard someone come into the kitchen.

She did not know who it was and before she could rise from her place on the floor, she heard a shot. She lowered herself to the floor in fear that whoever it was might see her.

She heard someone running and the kitchen door leading to the restaurant area was closed.

She waited a while longer and heard no sound, so she slowly rose from her place on the floor and looked around.

On the floor next to the stove was the body of man lying face down. There was a gun lying next to him. She approached the body slowly and bent down to see who was lying on the floor. She looked at the gun and then at the body again. She turned him over to see if she could help him and saw blood on the front of his shirt. She rose quickly from the floor and stepped back. Before she could call for help the door to the restaurant opened and several police officers came through. They told her not to move and she stood still.

One of the police officers grabbed her by the arms and pulled her away from the man lying on the floor. The other police officer checked the man on the floor and said he was dead. He picked up the gun and turned towards her. "Why did you kill him?"

Karen looked at him with wide eyes. "What?"

The police officer told the other officer holding Karen to take her away.

Karen went with them and was put in jail. The trial went quick. The man that was killed was a prominent businessman and there was a lot of press. The family wanted justice. She did not have any money for a lawyer so one was appointed and the trial, when it started, went quickly.

She was found guilty of murder. She had not seen her mother since she was imprisoned and tried to get someone to find out about her.

She tried to explain that her mother was ill and needed help. No one would listen to her and finally after two months in prison she received word that her mother had died.

Karen did not care what happened after that. She did not cry but kept to herself and did not speak to anyone anymore. No one would listen so why say anything.

****

Women's Prison 4 Months Later

One morning after she had been in the women's prison for four months the word came for all the women to gather in the cafeteria. She followed everyone down the hall and sat at one of the tables in the back of the room. She kept her head down. No one talked to her and she did not care.

The warden stood on one of the tables in the front of the cafeteria and announced that anyone that wanted to go as a bride to the Oregon Territory should stay behind. The rest could leave. Several young women stayed. The older ones left. One of them tried to stay but was laughed at.

Karen was not listening to what the Warden was saying. She was thinking of her mother and the times they had together. When she lifted her head, she was sitting alone at the table and there were only a few women left in the room. One of the guards was passing out papers for the women to fill out.

Karen looked at the paper in front of her, picked up the pen next to the form, and started filling out the information. They wanted her name, age, health, and a list of things she could do.

She filled it out and sat back. One of the guards picked up the paper and took it to the Warden who waited at the front of the room.

She did not move until one of the guards tapped her on the shoulder. She rose and followed the other women out of the room.

Two weeks later, she was taken from her cell and put in a wagon along with several other women. She did not care where she was going. They arrived at a boarding house in town and were given food and clean street clothes to wear. She did not ask any questions.

On The Train To Oregon

The next morning, they put chains on her wrists and around her ankles and took her to a train with the other women. The train left the station and Karen looked around. There were several women she remembered seeing in the prison sitting around the train car.

They were not allowed out of their seats during the trip except to use the laboratory. She did not know how long they traveled or where they were going.

Karen sat in her seat waiting for the train to pull out again when she saw that the other women were all getting off the train. She frowned and stood up and followed. They were led down the boardwalk of the station and into a room. Their chains were removed from their ankles but not their wrists.

They were then taken to a boarding house in town. She was given a room with another one of the women prisoners. The next morning, they were told to clean up and change into another dress.

She put on the dress and combed her hair. It was a matter of habit more than anything. She really did not care how she looked.

After breakfast, the women were all taken to a large building. Their chains were removed from around their wrists before they were led on to a stage at one end of a large room.

Karen looked up and saw a room full of men. She looked at each one. She was drawn to a large man in the back of the room. His hair touched his shoulders, and a beard covered his face. She stared at him until his eyes focused on her and he stared back. She stared into his eyes for a long time before lowering her head.

Kevin looked over the women on the stage. He needed a woman to cook and clean for him. He was tired of the whoring women in town and he needed someone to take care of his house. It was a crazy idea, but he could take one of these women, under contract for a year and use her as he pleased.

The marriage would not be complete until one year from the signing of the contract. He did not want a wife right now and he surely would not choose one of these women to have his children.

He looked at each one and stopped when he saw that one of them was staring at him. He was used to people staring at him because of his size. The woman did not falter or look away when he stared back at her.

He could not tell the color of her eyes from where he was, but she looked too small for what he needed. She would probably die the first week on his farm. It was hard work.

She finally lowered her head and he looked at the other women. A few looked like they would last at least the winter.

The Mayor came to the podium on the stage. "All right now. These women here have agreed to become wives for you men. I know there are more men here than women. Any man that sees something he likes, come forward and read through the papers they filled out."

Kevin moved forward with the rest of the men. He looked at the woman again, but she kept her head down and did not look up again.

Each of the women had a nametag around their necks so they could tell one from the other.

He noted that the woman that was staring at him was named Karen.

He read what she had written and moved away. For some reason he was not interested in any of the others. There was something about her that said she was the one he wanted.

The women on the stage were pushed back and told when their name was called they were to step forward.

Karen was pushed to the back of the group of women on the stage and waited.

Each woman stepped forward when her name was called and men in the room would bid on her. Cheers went up when the bidding was done, and another name was called.

Karen's name was the last to be called. She walked forward but did not look up. There was silence throughout the crowd. The Mayor asked for a bid but there was still silence. Karen looked up and saw that the men were staring at her.

She looked through the crowd until she saw the man she had seen at the back of the room. She said nothing but stared into his eyes. He was close enough for her to see that his eyes were a bright blue.

Kevin did not know why he did not say anything. He just stared at her and noticed her eyes were green.

When no one bid, the Mayor told the guard to take her back to the boardinghouse, then turned to the crowd. "Well now. All of you have signed your papers and each of you know the rules. One year from today, if the women do not fulfill their part of the bargain then she will be returned to prison. If you want to keep her then she will become your wife. Are there any questions?"

Kevin stepped forward. "What will happen to Karen?"

The Mayor looked at the woman being led off the stage. "She goes back to prison."

Kevin looked at the woman's back and said, "I bid two dollars."

Karen stopped and turned around. She stared at him and shook her head.

There was silence around the room. Not one of the women had questioned the bidding.

The Mayor looked at her. "You cannot disagree. If you do, you go back to prison. Is that what you want?"

Karen shook her head at the Mayor, turned to Kevin, and said, "It is too much."

Kevin stared at Karen and turned to the Mayor. "Three dollars."

The Mayor nodded and told the guard to bring Karen back to the center of the stage.

Kevin paid the three dollars and signed the paper. Karen was brought to the table and a pen was placed in her hand. She looked at Kevin for a moment before signing the paper.

Kevin led Karen out of the room and down the street to a hotel. He had reserved a room for two nights. It was a day's ride to his farm, and he came in yesterday.

He needed to get back. He would have only one night with the woman and then they would start back.

He read the paper she filled out and the information that was given to them about why she was in prison.

Kevin led Karen up to their room. He opened the door for her, and she walked through. He did not know why he did this. There was other woman that would do. He did not understand why he would want this one.

Karen looked around the room and stared at the bed. She knew he would expect her to sleep with him. She walked to the bed, sat down, and started talking off her shoes.

Kevin stared at Karen and asked, "What are you doing?"

Karen stopped and looked at him. "I thought…"

Kevin shook his head. "We need to get you some clothes and have dinner."

Karen nodded, laced her shoes, and stood.

Kevin opened the door and said, "Let's get you come clothes."

Karen followed him out and down the stairs. He took her to the Mercantile and told her to pick out some dresses, a coat, and other things she would need.

Karen walked around the store and picked out the least expensive dresses she could find, a nightgown, a comb, and brush. She put them on the counter and waited.

Kevin saw that she had picked the least expensive things in the store. "Is that all?"

Karen nodded.

Kevin turned to the women behind the counter. "We will need a coat for her and more clothes. Would you please help her?"

The woman nodded and Karen followed the woman around the store holding the items she selected. The woman selected undergarments, another dress, new shoes, stockings, a mirror, and another nightgown. Karen put them on the counter and looked at Kevin. "I will pay you back."

Kevin did not respond. He paid for the items, picked up the package, and went back to the hotel.

When he got to the lobby, he asked that a bath to be brought up to their room. He entered their room and put the packages on the bed. "I am going to check on the horses while you take your bath. Put on one of your new dresses and wait for me."

Karen nodded and sat in the chair by the window.

Kevin turned to leave then turned back to her. "Will you be here when I return?"

Karen nodded.

Kevin left and shook his head as he went down the hall. She was going to pay him back. Well, we will see how well she pays him tonight. It had been a long time since he had a woman.

Karen sat down in the water and closed her eyes. It had been a long time since she had taken a bath like this. The hotel staff had brought scented soap with the bath. She stayed in the water until it cooled. She had just stood up and wrapped the towel around her when the door opened, and Kevin walked in.

She gasped and pulled the towel tighter around her.

Kevin stared at her and said nothing. He swallowed hard. She was lovely. She was his and knew that he did not have to leave but the look on her face told him that he should. "I'll wait outside."

Karen nodded and got out of the tub when Kevin closed the door.

Kevin leaned against the wall next to the door to their room and shook his head. He was crazy.

There was no need for him to leave the room until she got dressed. He had paid for her and he had every right to watch her get dressed.

Karen dressed quickly. She did not want to anger Kevin. She opened the door and looked at him.

Kevin did not say anything but led the way out of the room to the dining room. They sat at a table by the window and ordered. When the food came, he was surprised at her manners.

After the meal, he took her back to the room. All of a sudden, he did not know what to do with her.

Karen sat in the chair by the window waiting for him to tell her what to do.

Kevin sat on the bed and looked at her. "I guess we could go to bed."

Karen nodded and started to unlace her shoes.

Kevin was angry for no reason. He did not like the way she acted. He stood up quickly and said, "Come on. I'll take you back to the boardinghouse."

Karen looked at him in surprise. "I have displeased you?"

"Damn it, woman. I need someone with life in her. Someone that can cook and clean and… other things. Not someone that won't even talk to me."

Karen stared at him and frowned. "What do you want me to say?"

Kevin sat down on the bed. "Tell me about yourself. You haven't even asked about my farm, what the house looks like, or anything."

"All right. My name is Karen Thompson. I am 24 years old. I have worked in the kitchens of the restaurants in New York since I was 15. My mother…" Karen stopped. The lump in her throat was hard to get past. She cleared her throat and continued. "Your farm. How big is it, what do your grow, and how big is your house?"

Kevin noticed that she changed the subject instead of finishing when she mentioned her mother. "I have almost a thousand acres, I use some acreage for growing crops and the rest is timberland. The house has three bedrooms."

Karen nodded and frowned. "Why would you need to buy a wife Mr. Andrews?"

"Call me Kevin. And I need a wife Karen not someone looking to dig their paws into my money."

Karen nodded. "What is it you want me to do?"

"Keep the house clean, cook the meals, feed the chickens, wash my clothes." He did not think he needed to state the obvious of sleeping together.

"Do you want children?"

Kevin shrugged. "Someday maybe. The contract is only for a year. I will probably find me a wife to have children with, in a couple of years."

Karen lowered her head so that he would not see how his words hurt her. She would be back in prison at the end of a year and he would find a respectable woman to be his wife.

The silence in the room was defining. Kevin took off his boots and started to unbutton his shirt. Karen began untying her shoes and undoing her dress. She turned away from him and pulled her nightgown out of the bag she had set on the floor.

"You won't need that tonight." Kevin said.

Karen swallowed hard and stood up. She took off her dress and petticoats but left her undergarments on. She went to the bed, pulled down the covers, and lay down.

Kevin removed the rest of his clothes and lay down beside her. He pulled her into his arms and could feel her stiffen. The papers on her said that she was having an affair with a businessman and killed him because he was going to go with someone else. She should know what he was going to do. He put his hand on her breast.

Karen closed her eyes. No one had ever touched her there before.

Kevin leaned over and kissed her. She lay still not knowing what to do. She wanted to touch him but did not know if he would like it.

Kevin pulled away and stared at her. "You don't have to play games with me Karen. I know you have had a man before. Part of the contract is that you will share my bed."

Karen stared at him. "I...." She took a deep breath and continued. "Yes."

Kevin kissed her again and she kissed him back. She liked kissing him.

Kevin pulled her chin down to open her mouth and put his tongue in her mouth to touch hers. He felt her stiffen, but she soon relaxed. He put his hand on her breast and felt her jerk. Kevin rolled onto his back and sighed. "You have never been with a man before have you?"

Karen was afraid he would send her away, but her mother also told her that a man would know if a woman had been with a man before. "No."

"Tell me what really happened back in New York. Why were you in prison."

Karen told him about the murder in the kitchen and being taken to jail. When she told him about her mother dying, she could not hold back the tears. "I...never got to see her again. There was no one to take care of her." Karen rolled away from Kevin and cried.

She was surprised when strong arms pulled her around to face him and hugged her. He held her and smoothed her hair with his hand. When she finished crying she tried to pull away, but he held her. "Go to sleep Karen."

Karen closed her eyes and slept with her head on his shoulder.

When Karen woke the next morning, Kevin was gone. She thought of the night before and knew she would be sent back to the boardinghouse and prison.

She put on the same dress they had given her and was gathering the clothes to take back to the store when Kevin entered the room. "What are you wearing that dress for?"

Karen looked at him. "After last night… I thought you were taking me back to the boardinghouse."

Kevin shook his head. "Change into one of your new dresses. After breakfast we have to leave for my farm."

Karen nodded and quickly changed into one of her new dresses. Kevin did not leave the room this time but sat on the bed and watched her. Maybe he signed a contract that might last more than a year.

The weather was nice all the way to Kevin's farm. She had never seen such beautiful trees and scenery before.

They arrived at his farm after dark. Kevin helped her down from the wagon and escorted her inside his house. He showed her around the house and ended at the room they would share.

Karen was nervous when she saw the big bed. He had waited last night. He could have taken her, but he did not. She would be considerate and do her best to please him in every way. This might be the only year she would ever have of freedom. There were so many memories she wanted to take away with her and one of them was to know what it felt like to lay in a man's arms.

Karen went to the kitchen when Kevin left to bring in their bags from the wagon.

Karen looked around the kitchen and smiled for the first time in months. It was large and fully stocked with food. She would enjoy cooking here.

Kevin returned and stood in the doorway looking at Karen in his kitchen. He wondered if she would be afraid of him tonight.

Karen turned and smiled at him. "Thank you Kevin."

Kevin was surprised and asked, "For what?"

"For giving me this year. I am going to make as many memories as I can."

Kevin nodded and sat at the table.

Karen had made coffee and brought him a cup. Kevin sipped the coffee carefully not knowing what to expect. It was the best he had ever had. "Won't you join me?"

Karen got a cup of coffee for herself and sat down at the table across from Kevin.

They were silent for a while. Karen spoke first. "Kevin. I am sorry about last night. Could we try again tonight?"

Kevin stared at her. "I'd like that." She did not say what he expected. He thought that she would want time to get to know him better. He was not sure if he could give her the time but now he would not have to find out.

Karen nodded and smiled at him.

Kevin finished his coffee and rose from the table. "I have to check on some things and I will be back later. You go on into bed."

Karen nodded and went to their room. She hung up her dresses and put her undergarments in the bottom dresser drawer that was empty.

She washed up and put on her nightgown. When Kevin came into the room, she was in bed waiting for him.

He approached her slowly and put out the light on the table next to the bed. He undressed and lay next to her under the covers. He pulled her into his arms and kissed her softly. He slowly made her his.

They made love twice during the night. He could not seem to get enough of her. He reached for her when he awoke in the predawn hours, but she was gone. He sat up quickly and put on his pants. He wondered if she had gone. He found her in the kitchen making bread. "What are you doing up so early?"

Karen smiled at him. "I am used to getting up early. When I worked in the restaurants I arrived before dawn and because I needed the extra money I worked extra hours, so I did not get home till after dark."

Kevin had not heard her talk so much since he met her. He wanted to ask her about last night but thought better of it. He knew most women did not talk about such things.

He turned to leave but stopped when she said, "Kevin. Last night was wonderful. Thank you."

Kevin stared at her and only nodded. He finished getting dressed for the day and Karen had breakfast ready when he came back to the kitchen.

"What do you want me to do today?"

"I have to check on some things and I should be back in time for lunch. I can show you around the farm this afternoon."

Karen nodded. "Would it be all right if I looked around outside while you are gone?'

Kevin nodded and left after breakfast. Karen had already started the wash and hung it on the line soon after he left. She walked around the house and went to the barn. She had never lived in the country before and wanted to have as many memories as possible in this year of freedom. She knew that Kevin would send her back when the year was up. He said he wanted a real wife to have his children.

The barn was big, and she met a young man, who was cleaning out the stalls. They talked for a while and Karen went back to the house. She had lunch ready when Kevin arrived. After lunch, he hitched up the wagon and took her around his farm. She asked questions and enjoyed the time with him.

When they returned to the house, she started dinner while Kevin went to his study.

Over the next few months, they would have meals together and talk in the evenings for a while, and then Kevin would go to his study. They made love every night and Karen was happy. She would tend the garden behind the house, do her chores outside in the morning, keep the house clean, and fix his meals.

Karen had been on the farm for eight months when there was an accident at the lumber mill on Kevin's property. He was badly hurt, and the men brought him home in a wagon.

Karen knew something was wrong when she saw the wagon. She knew Kevin had been hurt. She ran to the wagon when it stopped in the yard and saw him lying in the back. He was as still as death. She knew he was still alive, she felt it. "Bring him inside but be careful."

Four men carried him into their room and Karen asked what happen as she was taking off his clothes.

The foreman, Robert, answered. "There was an accident. One of the piles of lumber came lose and fell on him."

Karen finished taking off his clothes and was checking for wounds. "You are the foreman aren't you?"

Robert nodded. "Yes ma'am."

"Find out how the lumber got loose. We don't want this to happen again."

Robert nodded and left. The other men stayed, and Karen said. "Thank you for bringing him home. Is there a doctor anywhere near here?"

The men shook their heads. Jason answered. "No ma'am. The closest doctor is three days ride."

Karen nodded and went to the kitchen for hot water. The men followed. "One of you ride for the doctor. Is there a store in town that sells medicine?"

Jason answered. "Yes ma'am. The Mercantile has some medicine."

"Good. I am going to give you a list of what I want. Ride as fast as you can."

Jason nodded. Karen made out a list of what she wanted and handed it to him.

Karen went back into the bedroom where Kevin lay on the bed and began to wash the dirt and dust from him. He moaned once but did not wake up. The extent of his injuries was minor on the outside, but Karen knew that he might have had some internal injuries. She had seen one of those lumber pile's months ago. Kevin had told her how dangerous it would be if they fell on anyone.

Karen bathed him, put some salve on the cuts and bruises she could see and covered him up. All she could do was keep him warm, give him some water, and wait for the medicine she asked for from town and the doctor.

Kevin woke up some hours later in great pain. Karen did not have anything to give him, so she got the bottle of whisky, he kept in his study, and gave him some.

Jason arrived back at the ranch at sunup with the medicine she asked for. She gave Kevin some laudanum for the pain. She made some broth to give him and watched him for two days before he finally opened his eyes.

He looked at her sitting beside the bed. Karen quickly sat on the bed next to him. "How are you feeling?"

Kevin thought about what happened. He was checking the lines on one of the lumber piles and next thing he knew the lumber was rolling over him. He could feel pain in his back and across his chest, but he felt nothing in his legs. He lifted his left arm and then his right then tried to move his feet. They would not move. He looked at Karen. "My legs."

Karen went to the foot of the bed and drew back the covers. She touched his feet. "Can you feel this?"

Kevin shook his head.

Karen moved her hands up the calves of his legs. "This?"

Kevin shook his head again.

Karen stood back, looked at his legs, and nodded. "Okay. You must have injured your legs. They do not feel broken. I checked them before when they brought you home. I have sent for the doctor. He should be here tomorrow." She covered him back up and went to get him some broth.

Kevin watched her go and became angry. She acted as if she did not even care. Was she hoping that he would keep her after her year was over? That he would need her to take care of him?

Karen returned to Kevin a short time later. "Here is some broth. We need to keep your strength up. I am sure in a couple of days your legs will be better. I sent Jason into town right away for some medicine for the pain and the doctor should be here at any time."

Kevin began to relax a little and lose his anger. Maybe he was angry for no reason. Maybe in a few days, he could feel his legs.

The doctor examined him and told him to rest. His back was damaged in the accident. Only time will tell if the feelings would come back in his legs. Karen talked to the doctor before he left.

She told him about the doctor in New York that was looking after her mother and some things she remembered the doctor saying about one of his patients that was like Kevin. The doctor agreed that the exercises she wanted to do would be a good idea but wait about a month before she tried them. His body needed time to heal.

After a month passed, from the time of his injury, Kevin grew concerned and took it out on Karen. One day she had had enough. She put her hands on her waist and stared at him. "Kevin. That is enough. It is going to take time for your legs to heal. I am going to keep rubbing them each day like I learned from the doctor years ago. You could try and help me by being a better patient."

Kevin nodded.

Since his pain had lessened when he moved, and the doctor said he could do the exercises, Karen asked one of the men to build a form of exercise structure. He would exercise his arms in the morning. The ropes were attached to his feet in the afternoon, and she would raise each leg one at a time. Each week she would add more weights.

Karen had been with Kevin for nine months now and realized she was pregnant. It must have happened just before he had the accident.

If she were lucky, he would be walking in a few months and she would not be showing before her year was over.

She did not tell him. He had enough to worry about.

Robert would come in each evening and talk about the mill and the crops. Karen left them alone.

After two weeks of exercising his arms and legs, he moved his left foot. Karen stopped and stared at his left foot.

She lowered it to the bed and walked to the foot of the bed. "Kevin, move your left foot."

Kevin looked at his left foot and tried to move it. It moved a little. He tried to move the right foot and it moved. There was a pain in his back when he moved them but not much.

Karen kept to the schedule of working his legs each day but after they exercised them with the ropes, she would bend his leg and put his foot on her chest. "Now push hard."

Kevin would push and each day he could see that he could push more.

Karen came into his room three weeks later with crutches. "Okay. Let's see if you can stand up."

Kevin threw back the covers and pulled up on the crutches. He could feel his feet on the floor. He moved the right foot forward and back then the left. He smiled at Karen. He put the right foot out, put all his weight on it, and moved forward. He moved the left foot forward and repeated the process as he slowly walked around the room on the crutches. There was a pain in his lower back but not too much.

Karen smiled. He would be walking before she left. She put her hand on her stomach and thought of the baby she carried. She wondered what would happen to it when she returned to prison. Would they let her keep it?

Kevin saw that Karen was frowning. "Karen. What's wrong?"

Karen shook her head and smiled. "Nothing. How do your legs feel? Any pain?"

Kevin shook his head. "Only a little in my back but I think if we do this every day it won't be long before I can walk again."

Karen nodded.

The doctor came by and told him to take it slow. He followed Karen into the kitchen. He told her that he did not believe the exercises would work when she first suggested them.

He knew about the contract and said that if it did not work out and she needed a job and wanted to be his nurse he would speak for her. Karen nodded and the doctor left.

The next two weeks went fast as Kevin walked more each day on the crutches. He continued the exercises each day with his legs and arms. He pulled down on the ropes with his legs and could feel the pain in his back lessen each day.

It was only a week before Karen would have to return to the prison. She did not mention it to Kevin, and he did not say anything. They had been making love each night for two weeks now and she knew she loved him. She did not realize that there were so many ways to make love.

She was only four months pregnant and not showing very much. Kevin only thought that she had gained a little weight. She would be able to leave without him noticing.

The day before she was to leave to go back to prison, a letter was delivered addressed to Kevin. She put the letter in the study and went to fix dinner. Kevin walked into the kitchen on his crutches. In another week or two, he would not need them at all.

She told Kevin about the letter and set the table.

Kevin read the letter and smiled. Karen had been cleared of all charges. She was free. Then he frowned. She was free to leave him. He would tell her in the morning. He wanted at least one more night with her.

They ate in silence during the meal and went to bed early. They made love twice during the night. In the morning while Kevin was still sleeping, Karen put on the dress they gave her at the boardinghouse and hitched the wagon. She took nothing else. She would only take what she came with.

When Kevin woke, he found her side of the bed empty. A fear that she had left came over him. Then he relaxed. She was just an early riser.

When he went into the kitchen, she was not there. He saw a letter on the kitchen table and sat down to read it.

"My dearest Kevin.

Thank you for a wonderful year. I have some wonderful memories to take with me. You are free now to find the wife you can love and to give you children. I love you and wish you only good things in life.

Always Karen."

Kevin put down the letter. She was gone. Kevin read the part again, where she said she loved him. Well, if she loved him, why did she leave?

Kevin went into their room and saw that all the dresses he had bought her were still there. He opened the dresser drawer she used and found her undergarments were still there. She had taken nothing. No, Kevin thought, she had taken his heart.

He had to stop her. He rushed to the barn and saddled his horse. He threw his crutches to the ground and rode as hard as he could to catch up with her.

Karen was halfway to town when she heard a sound behind her. Someone was coming. She did not stop but kept going.

Kevin pulled up alongside of Karen's wagon. "Good morning. Nice day for a ride."

Karen nodded but did not answer.

"I didn't get my breakfast this morning."

Karen could stand the pretense no longer. She pulled in on the reigns of the horses and stopped the wagon. "Kevin today our year is up. I am going back. You are free now to marry a woman you can love and give you children."

Kevin stared at her and said, "You are also free Karen. The letter I received yesterday was an inquiry into your trial. They found the woman that killed the man and she confessed."

Karen stared at Kevin with wide eyes. "I am free?"

Kevin nodded and cleared his throat. "Did you mean it when you said you loved me?"

Karen nodded. "Yes."

Kevin got down from his horse, walked to the wagon without his crutches, and climbed up next to her. "Then let's go home wife."

Karen stared at him and then hugged him. "I can stay?"

Kevin kissed her and that was all answer she needed.

Later that night after they made love, she told him about the baby.

Love's Sweet Song

"Doubt thou the stars are fire,
Doubt that the sun doth move,
Doubt truth to be a liar,
But never doubt I love."
Hamlet

To Everyone that believes in Love and for those that need more convincing.

Marlina was born with a birthmark on her right cheek. It was not a large mark, but it made her face appear scarred and she was hidden away on the family estate.

She did not have to attend the classes her sisters did because no one would want to marry her. She was left to help the servants and run along after the servant's children. When she turned twelve she spent almost all of her days with the horses. She loved to ride and learned how to tend them.

When she was eighteen she wanted to be in the choir but with her face scared like it was she would be in front of everyone to see and her family would not have that. She went to the pastor and asked him if she could sing in church. The pastor knew of her family's treatment of her and also knew that they would not allow her to sing in front of the congregation.

He also knew that she had a lovely voice. He had heard her when she came to church. Her family did not attend often but she was at every service. It was God's way of making up for the scar on her face. They could use makeup to cover the scar, but her family would still know who she was and remove her from the choir.

The pastor came up with an elaborate plan to put a black wig over her blond hair and use makeup to cover the scar. She would wear a veil of white over her face to cover her appearance. She could sing songs at special services.

Marlina was excited and practiced the song she was to sing at the Easter service. No one knew it was her when she entered the church in her disguise. She sat on the first row and the pastor introduced her as Miss Margaret. He did not give any further introduction. The congregation was curious.

When Marlina had finished her song, everyone was silent. The pastor looked out on his congregation and could see that they were all spellbound by the beautiful voice they had just heard.

Marlina excited the church through the side door after she had finished her song. After the service, the pastor was asked about the woman who sang. He told them that she was a distant relative and that she would return soon to sing for them again.

Every Sunday several members of the congregation asked about her and when she would sing again.

The pastor asked Marlina to sing at least once a month at the service. She agreed and by the time Christmas came there were so many people in the church in hopes of hearing her sing that there were not enough places for everyone to sit. They were standing in the isle, along the outer side of the pews, along the walls and outside on the lawn.

Jason Matthew, the Earl of Hastings, was in the congregation. He had heard about the mysterious lady that sang in the church and wanted to hear her sing. He sat in the first row and waited for her to appear.

Marlina came out after the sermon on Christmas Eve and everyone became silent. All eyes were on her and she sang her song. She was leaving when everyone stood up and applauded her. She turned back to them and curtsied. Many asked for her to sing another song. She looked at the Pastor and he nodded. She turned to the choir and the organ player and told them the song she would like to sing. When she turned back to the congregation, they all sat down and silently waited for the angel to sing.

Marlina sang her favorite Christmas song and then left through the side door of the church.

Jason rushed quickly out of the church to speak with her. He had never heard anyone with a voice as lovely as hers. He searched but did not find her. He went back into the church and waited to speak with the Pastor.

The Pastor said he could not give him any information about her. He tried to answer the Earl's questions without lying but it was hard. The Pastor knew others were listening to their conversation and soon took the Earl aside.

"My Lord, I cannot tell you who the young lady is. I am bound by a confidence. To tell you the truth her family would not approve. I am sorry."

Jason nodded and asked when she would sing again. The Pastor said that she would sing again in three Sundays. Jason left the church without any more questions. He would be back in three Sundays to hear her again. Maybe he could catch up with her then.

Marlina watched the man that ran after her. She could tell the way he was dressed that he was of the ton. She sank back into the shadows and hid from him. When he left, she ran to her room the Pastor let her use and changed out of her wig and veil. She scrubbed her face of the makeup she used and changed back into her plain brown dress.

When she arrived home the servants were all talking about the beautiful woman that sang at the service. They were all trying to guess who she was. She passed the parlor and heard her family discussing the woman they had heard singing in church. Her sister Ester was getting married in two weeks and she wanted the woman to sing at her wedding. She was pleading with her father to find the woman and make her sing for her.

Marlina smiled and went to her room. She would of course sing at her sister's wedding. She would talk to the Pastor next week.

Jason received an invitation to a wedding the next week. The wedding was to be held at the same church that he heard the mysterious woman sing. He did not usually attend weddings, but he was hoping that the woman would sing.

He arrived at the church and asked the Pastor if Margaret was going to sing. The Pastor informed him that she was. Jason took his seat and waited.

Marlina was not invited to the wedding, which was a good thing for she could not sit with the family and sing.

She came out and sang her song then left through the side door of the church. She was in a hurry to get away before any of her family recognized her and did not see Jason rush after her.

Jason spotted her rushing down a hallway away from the chapel and called to her. Marlina stopped in surprise. She kept her head lowered and did not look at the man who called after her. "I am sorry sir, but I am in a hurry."

Jason stopped a short distance away from her. "I have been wanting to meet you. You have a lovely voice."

Marlina felt warm when she heard his voice. She looked at him and caught her breath. He was beautiful. She also noticed that he was the man who ran after her at Christmas. "Thank you sir. Now if you will excuse me I am in a hurry."

Jason stopped her when she would have fled. "I would like to meet with you. Talk to you."

Marlina shook her head. As much as she would like to know him, she knew that he would not want to know her. "I am sorry sir, but I must go."

Marlina ran into the night but Jason did not follow. He knew that she would sing again soon. He would keep coming back until she agreed to see him. Anyone with a voice that lovely was worth coming back for.

Jason was in the congregation the next Sunday when Marlina sang again. She saw him as she entered. She also knew that he would follow her again.

She did not run away this time when he rushed out of the church after her. She waited and curtsied to him. "I see that you are persistent sir. There is a reason that I must keep my identify a secret. Please understand."

Jason nodded and said,. "The Pastor told me that your family would not approve. Is that why you hid your face?"

Marlina did not want to tell him the reason she hid her face was also because of the scar on her right cheek. She wanted to see him and speak with him, but she could not lie to him and give him any false hopes. "That is only part of the reason. I am...scarred. No one would hear me if I did not wear this disguise."

Jason did not respond. Marlina took his response as a sign that he did not want to see her again and she turned to leave.

Jason put his hand on her arm. "Would you ride with me tomorrow?"

Marlina looked at his hand on her arm and could feel the warmth seep into her skin. "I am sorry sir, but you do not want to be seen with me and you cannot call on me at my home." She put her hand over his and said, "You do not want to embarrass yourself sir."

Marlina ran away from him and by the time she arrived home, her makeup was running down her face with her tears.

Jason watched her runaway and did not chase after her. He would see her again. And the next time he would convince her to ride with him. He would do some inquiries and find this woman.

He knew that she was of a well to do family by the way she carried herself and spoke to him. She gave herself away when she said that he should not call on her at her home. That meant that her family was a member of the ton. He also knew that she lived close to the church for she ran into the forest not to a waiting carriage.

Jason had a plan, and he would follow it out. He smiled and left the church. He spent the next few weeks making inquiries and found out who the lady was. Her name was Marlina. It had to be her. She had a birthmark on her right cheek and from what he uncovered she was not well received by her family. She was treated more like a servant than the daughter of the Duke of Westerling.

Marlina knew that the man who chased after her twice would be waiting for her the next time she sang. She was nervous but also knew that he would not follow her.

When she arrived at the church three weeks later, she was surprised to see the Pastor so excited and he pulled her into his office. "Marlina. Do you know who is going to be in the congregation this afternoon? The Queen."

Marlina gasped. She did not know what to do. "I cannot sing today. You must tell everyone."

The Pastor shook his head. "You must sing. She told me that she came all this way from London to hear you. She has heard so much about you that she wants to invite you to the palace to sing for her."

Marlina shook her head. "No. You do not understand. She must not find out who I am. I cannot go to the palace or anywhere. If I do, my family will know, and they will stop me. How can I sing without my disguise? No one would listen to me."

The Pastor could see that Marlina was afraid and tried to calm her. "Marlina. You have been given a rare and beautiful gift. Please do not hide it from the world. If you must keep your disguise then we will think of something."

Marlina knew that her singing had brought more people to the church. The money the Pastor was collecting, each Sunday she sang, he was giving it to the people of the village. She nodded and the Pastor smiled.

Marlina knew that she had to sing so she went out after the Pastor's sermon and sang more beautifully than she had ever sung before. Her voice was perfect.

She noticed that the man she had met on two different occasions was in the congregation sitting next to the Queen. She knew he would not chase after her again. She would leave as soon as the song was over.

She did not get the chance to run because the Queen stood as soon as her song ended and approached her.

Marlina curtsied to the Queen. She could not leave until the Queen dismissed her. This was going to be the last time she would ever sing in the church. She asked one last request. "Your majesty. I...would like to sing one more song before..." Marlina swallowed hard and continued. "Please. I believe it is your favorite."

The Queen smiled at her and nodded. She returned to her seat.

Marlina approached the organ player and told him what to play. Then she returned to face the audience. Since she knew that it was her last time to sing for them she wanted them to know who she was. She took off her wig and veil. She could hear the collective gasps of the congregation, but no one left. She swallowed hard and nodded to the organ player.

Marlina did not look at anyone while she sang her last song. When it ended, everyone was silent. Marlina curtsied to the Queen, looked at the man next to her, and ran from the church.

She did not know anyone was following her until she stopped in the forest because she was crying so hard that she could no longer see where she was going.

Jason followed Marlina out of the church and through the forest. She would not get away from him again.

He found her sitting under a tree crying. He approached her quietly and knelt down to touch her arm.

Marlina jumped at the touch of something on her arm and saw that it was a hand. She knew that hand. She looked into the man's face, quickly pulled her hair to cover her right cheek, and looked away.

Jason turned her face back to him and moved her hair away from her cheek. He studied her face and then smiled. "You are lovely."

Marlina tried to pull away from him but he held her face towards him. "The scar on your cheek is nothing. Your eyes are as beautiful as your voice." He rose and held out his hand. "Come the Queen would like to speak with you."

Marlina took his hand and left him help her up. "You are kind sir but…" She did not finish for her father appeared behind Jason. She saw her father only a second before he pushed Jason away and slapped her so hard she fell to the ground. "How dare you. How dare you embarrass us like that and to find you here like this."

Jason moved to stand between Marlina and her father. "How dare you strike this woman? Who are you?"

Marlina's father stepped back and asked, "I am her father. I can do as I please. Who the devil are you?"

Jason smiled and said, "I am the Earl of Hastings, first cousin to the Queen."

Marlina gasped and tried to get up off the ground. Jason turned to help her up. Marlina curtsied to the Earl. "My Lord. Please. I thank you but I must go home now."

Marlina's father said, "You do not have a home." And turned around and walked away.

Marlina hung her head. She took a deep breath and started walking back to the church. She knew that the Pastor would help her. There were things she could do around the church and probably stay there for a while. She knew that when she sang this last time that her life would change but she did not think that her father would turn her out.

Jason followed Marlina back to the church. He did not speak because he knew that Marlina would not listen. Also, he knew that he could not offer her a position in his household. It would damage her reputation.

He would speak to the Queen on her behalf. Maybe she could become a part of the court.

The Queen had left the church by the time they returned. Marlina turned to the Earl and said, "Thank you sir for your kind words and your protection. I will speak with the Pastor. I am sure that I may stay here for a while."

Jason stopped her when she turned to leave. "Marlina. I wish there were something I could do." Jason felt responsible for the turn of events.

Marlina shook her head. "That is not necessary. I will be fine."

"Marlina. Will ride with me tomorrow?"

Marlina shook her head. "I am sorry My Lord. I have nothing now but what you see. My horse, my clothes, everything is gone. You are kind to offer but I must speak with the Pastor." Marlina curtsied and left him watching her walk away.

Jason did not want to leave her. After all that had happened in the forest, she did not blame him for her being turned out of her home. The scar on her cheek was invisible to him. All he saw was the beauty of her eyes, heard the lovely sound of her voice and felt her touch his soul when she sang. He felt emptiness as he watched her walk away. To never look into her eyes again, hear her voice or feel the power of her song was too much to bear.

Marlina found the Pastor and told him what had happened in the forest. He told her she could stay as long as she wished.

Marlina nodded and followed the Pastor as he led her down the hallway to her new room. She asked him about clothes to wear and he showed her a room of clothes that had been donated for the villagers. She chose a simple rust colored dress and took it back to her room.

She joined the Pastor for dinner then returned to her room. She cried half the night but the next morning she woke with determination. She would be all right. She would prove herself worthy to stay at the church. The next week went quietly. She practiced her singing with the choir and on Sunday the church was full of people that had come to hear her sing. They did not care about the scar on her cheek.

She stood before the congregation without her disguise. She had put some makeup on her cheek and the scar was barely visible.

She knew the Earl of Hastings was in the church but did not look at him. She was too ashamed for what he witnessed in the forest. She sang her song and the congregation all stood and cheered.

Jason found her sitting in the gardens behind the church. She stood and curtsied to him. "My Lord. I hoped you like the sermon."

Jason smiled at her. "Call me Jason and I came to hear you sing."

Marlina smiled and sat down on the bench. "Thank you sir…Jason. You are very kind."

Jason sat next to Marlina and talked with her for an hour before he announced he had to leave but before he left he said, "Marlina. I am having a party next Friday. Would you attend and sing for my guests?"

Marlina lost her smile. "I…I am sorry…Jason, but as you know I have nothing to wear to such a party."

"Do not worry. You are the same size as my sister. I am sure she has a gown you can wear. Please Marlina. It would mean a great deal to me."

Marlina smiled. "If she would not mind loaning me something to wear, then of course I will sing at your party."

Jason smiled and kissed the back of her hand before he left.

Marlina watched him leave and raised the back of her hand, where he had kissed her to her lips.

Jason came to see her every afternoon during the week. He sent a carriage to pick Marlina up at the church early on Friday. When she arrived at Jason's estate his sister, Lynette met her. She was excited about the evening and took Marlina to a beautiful room to change for the party. Since it was early, Lynette ordered some tea and talked with Marlina for a long time.

Lynette instructed the maid to fix Marlina's hair and brought her the most beautiful dress she had ever seen. The emerald gown matched her eyes and she put makeup on the scar. Lynette said you could hardly notice the scar and Marlina smiled.

Jason knocked on Marlina's bedroom door to escort her to the party. When Marlina opened the door, she expected to find Lynette standing there and was surprised to see Jason. He looked beautiful. She must have said it out loud because he laughed and said, "You my dear are the one who is beautiful."

Marlina curtsied and said, "Thank you my Lord."

Jason held out his arm, Marlina put her gloved hand on his arm, and he led her down the staircase. Marlina was surprised when he kept her with him as the guests began to arrive. That position was for the lady of the estate. She thought Lynette would be the one to stand by his side to greet the guests.

After the guests had arrived, Jason took her to the ballroom and led the first dance with her. She learned how to dance while watching her sisters. This was the first time she had danced with anyone. When she told him this, she knew she had made a mistake for he grew angry. He left her with his sister after the dance was over and did not return to her until it was time for her to sing.

Marlina knew that she would leave right after her song. He acted as though he was still angry with her. She would miss him. She had fallen in love with him over the past week and she knew that he would never marry anyone that looked like she did.

Jason led her out into the gardens. Marlina was surprised. She thought it was time for her to sing.

Jason led her away from the couples in the garden and found a quiet place by the fountain. He knew he did not act proper when she told him that this was the first time she had danced and learned from watching her sisters when they had their lessons. He also knew that she knew he was angry, but she did not understand why. He gestured for her to sit on the bench near the fountain and stood next to her.

"Marlina, I must apologize for my behavior earlier. I did not mean to upset you. I was not angry with you but the way in which your family has treated you."

Marlina nodded and said nothing.

Jason sighed and sat next to her. He watched her closely when he said, "The reason I asked you here tonight was not only to have you sing but to announce my engagement."

Marlina's eyes widened at the announcement of his engagement. She turned her head away quickly. "I...congratulations my lord." Then she looked at him and frowned. "But I stood by your side to greet your guests and danced the first dance with you. Isn't that the place of your intended?"

Jason smiled at her and said, "Yes."

Marlina's eyes widened again. "You...I mean...what..."

Jason laughed and kissed her for the first time. Marlina put her arms around his neck and kissed him back. Jason ended the kiss and asked, "I love you Lina. Do you think you could learn to love me enough to marry me?"

"I love you too." Marlina turned her head away. "But Jason what about...I mean you should marry someone that you..." she turned back to face him and asked, "What about my scar. It..."

Jason did not let her finish. "Sweetheart. It is hardly noticeable. Your family was wrong in how they treated you. You are a beautiful woman that I love desperately. Will you marry me Lina? Can I announce our engagement tonight?"

Marlina smiled. "Yes my love. Let us announce our engagement and then I will sing for you."

And Marlina did sing for him. She never took her eyes off him while she sang her song after Jason announced their engagement.

Marlina's family came to the wedding but she did not acknowledge them nor allow her father to give her away. She asked the Pastor if he could escort her down the aisle and still perform the ceremony. He said he would be honored to. Jason talked with her father for only a few moments after the wedding.

When she asked him later what he said to him Jason replied, "I told him that you belonged to me now and that it was up to you if he or his family was ever to see you again."

Marlina kissed her husband. No one had ever stood up for her before. She loved him so much.

Marlina and Jason had a long and happy life together. She sang often for the Queen and the court.

Marlina was excited about the party that evening. All of her family would be there. They had been arriving for the past two days.

Jason kissed her and walked with her down the staircase to meet the gathered guests and family.

He led her into the ballroom, and everyone cheered. Jason quieted everyone and turned to his wife. "My love. I have to tell you a secret that I have been carrying for 50 years. I fell in love with you the first time I heard you sing. When I met you, I fell in love with you again by looking into the most beautiful green eyes I had ever seen. And then again as I came to know your generosity, kindness, and gentle nature. You have given me more love than any man could want or dream of having."

Marlina kissed her husband on the cheek and heard the applause and cheers. "You my love have given me more than I had ever hoped for or dreamed possible. I fell in love with you the first time you touched my arm. Again, when you kissed my hand and again and again over the years with your thoughtfulness."

Jason pulled her to him and kissed her long and deep. The cheers and applause faded into the background as she put her arms around his neck and kissed him back.

Jason ended the kiss and said, "Now my love since we have all of our children and grandchildren present would do us the honor of singing a song?"

Marlina smiled and moved to stand near the piano. She was 69 years old, but her voice was as beautiful as it was when she was 19. Everyone applauded when she had finished. Her daughter Marianna had been granted her gift and they sang a song together. Then everyone joined in to raise their voices to several songs she had taught them over the years.

Later that night Jason held Marlina and thanked God for giving her to him. Marlina held onto Jason and thanked God for the gift of song that brought her to him.

www.ingramcontent.com/pod-product-compliance
Lightning Source LLC
Chambersburg PA
CBHW061539050726

47593CB00002B/839